MERCER MAYER'S CRITTER KIDS® ADVENTURES

GOLDEN EAGLE

A GRAPHIC NOVEL ADVENTURE

#3

Copyright © 2006 © 1995 Mercer Mayer Ltd.
Text for Page 32 © 2006 School Specialty Publishing.
Published by School Specialty Publishing, a member of the School Specialty Family.
A Big Tuna Trading Company, LLC/J. R. Sansevere Book

Written by Erica Farber/J. R. Sansevere
Special thanks to Julie Collier, Native American Raptor Rehabilitator

ISBN 0-7696-4764-2

1 2 3 4 5 6 7 8 9 10 PHX 11 10 09 08 07 06

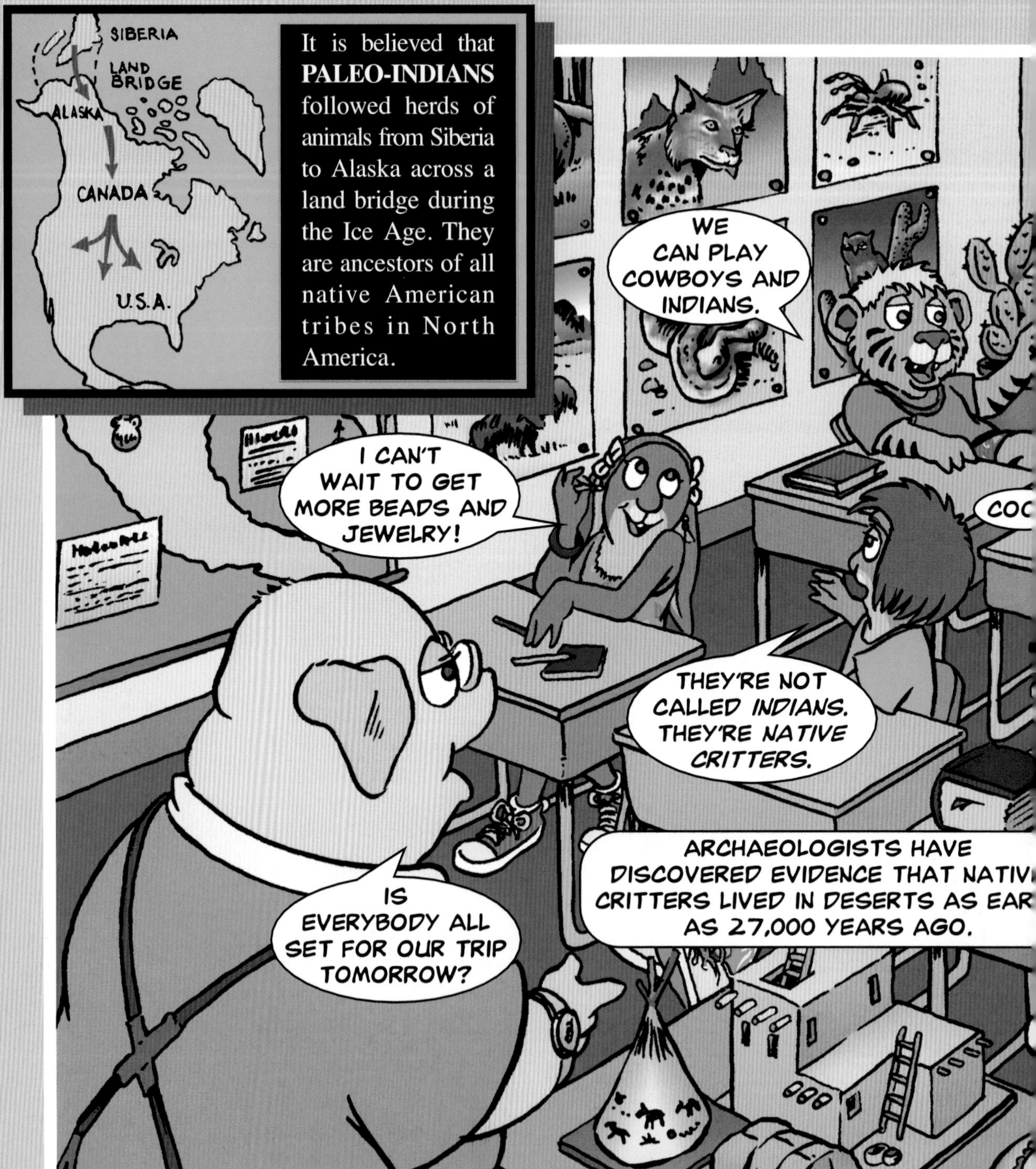
SIBERIA
LAND BRIDGE
ALASKA
CANADA
U.S.A.
It is believed that PALEO-INDIANS followed herds of animals from Siberia to Alaska across a land bridge during the Ice Age. They are ancestors of all native American tribes in North America.
WE CAN PLAY COWBOYS AND INDIANS.
I CAN'T WAIT TO GET MORE BEADS AND JEWELRY!
THEY'RE NOT CALLED INDIANS. THEY'RE NATIVE CRITTERS.
IS EVERYBODY ALL SET FOR OUR TRIP TOMORROW?
ARCHAEOLOGISTS HAVE DISCOVERED EVIDENCE THAT NATIV
CRITTERS LIVED IN DESERTS AS EAR
AS 27,000 YEARS AGO.

The Critter Kids were going on a class trip to visit Coyote Canyon, a Native Critter desert reservation.

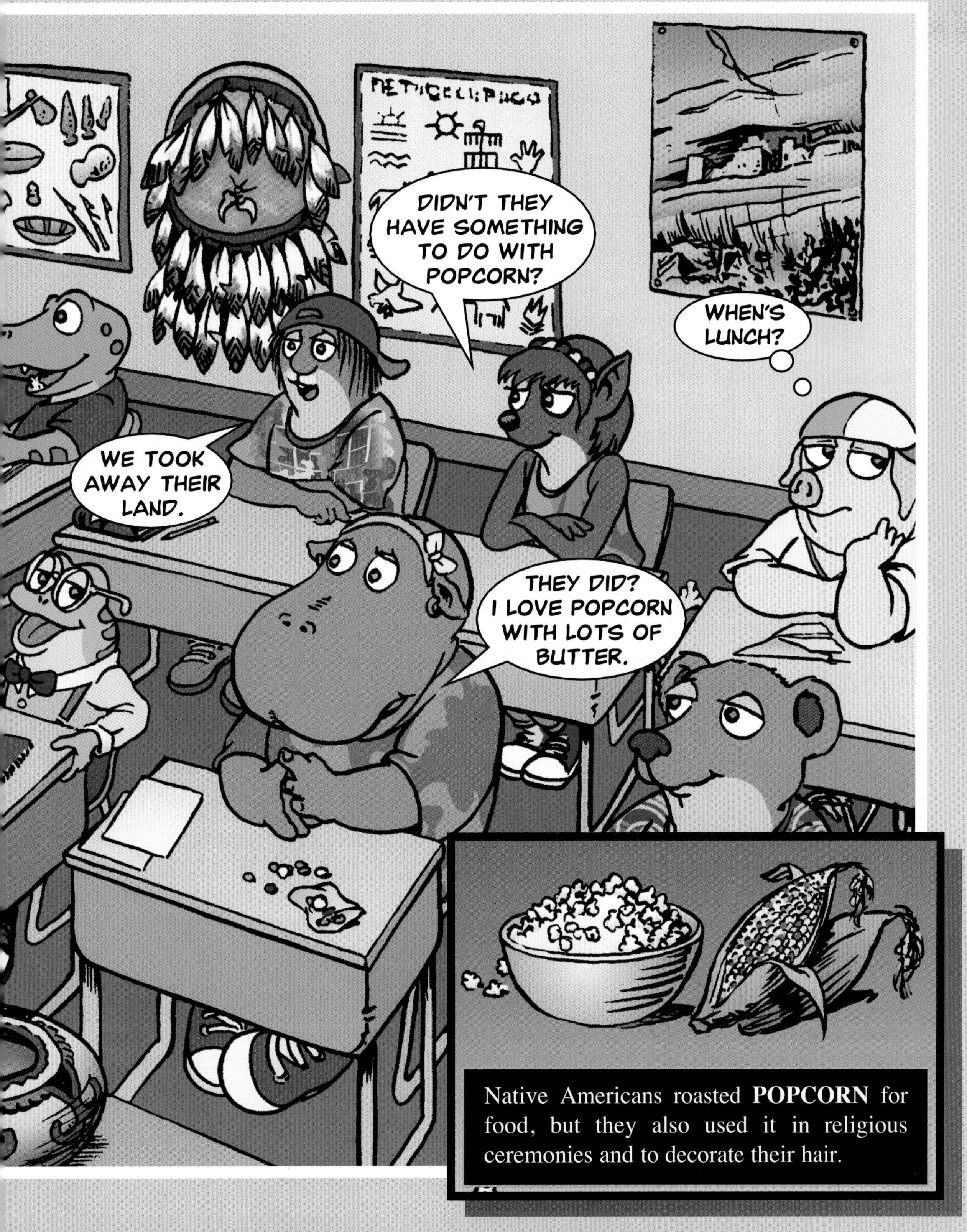
DIDN'T THEY HAVE SOMETHING TO DO WITH POPCORN?
WHEN'S LUNCH?
WE TOOK AWAY THEIR LAND.
THEY DID? I LOVE POPCORN WITH LOTS OF BUTTER.

Native Americans roasted **POPCORN** for food, but they also used it in religious ceremonies and to decorate their hair.

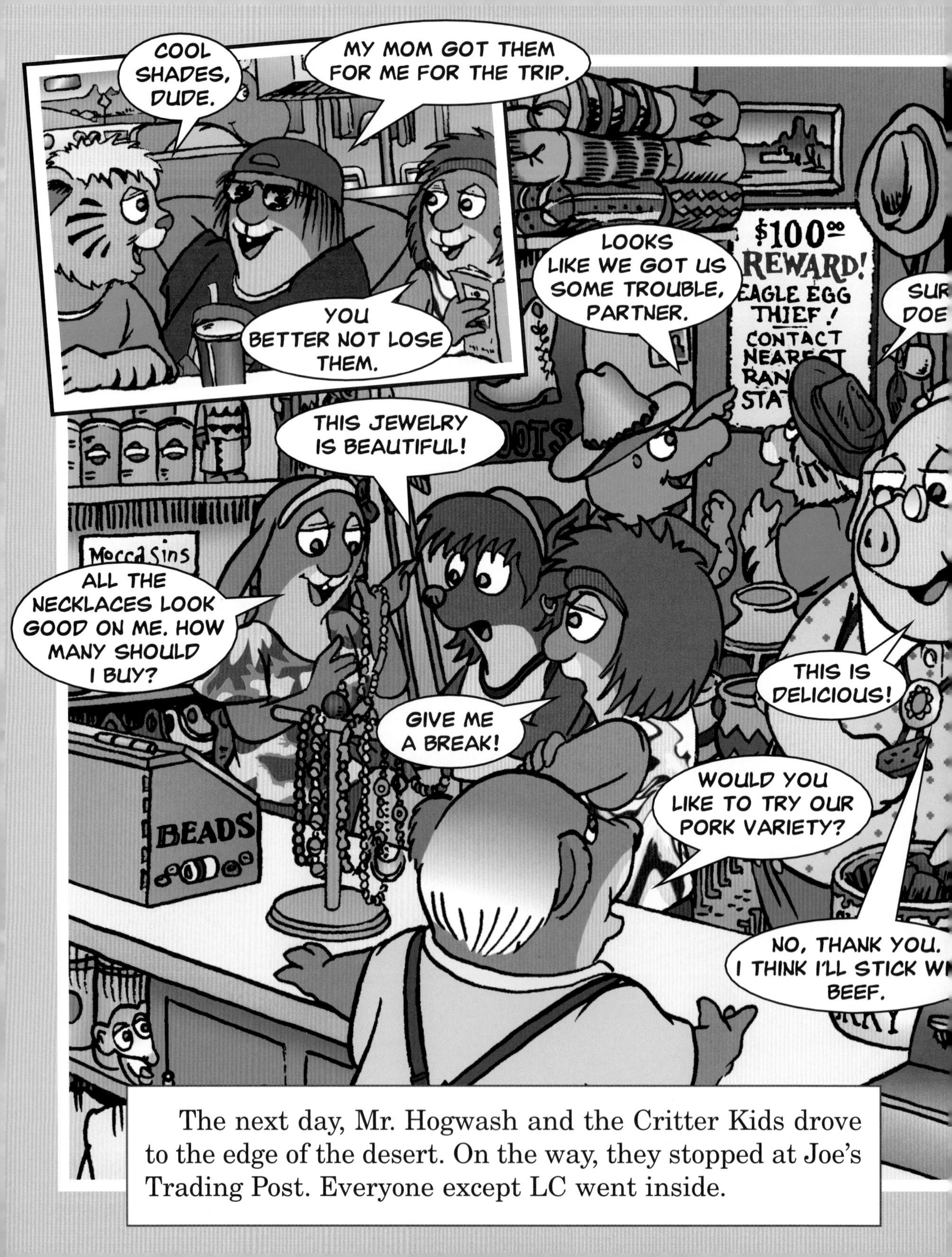
COOL SHADES, DUDE.
MY MOM GOT THEM FOR ME FOR THE TRIP.
YOU BETTER NOT LOSE THEM.
LOOKS LIKE WE GOT US SOME TROUBLE, PARTNER.
$100.00 REWARD! EAGLE EGG THIEF! CONTACT NEAREST RAN STAT
THIS JEWELRY IS BEAUTIFUL!
Moccasins
ALL THE NECKLACES LOOK GOOD ON ME. HOW MANY SHOULD I BUY?
GIVE ME A BREAK!
THIS IS DELICIOUS!
WOULD YOU LIKE TO TRY OUR PORK VARIETY?
NO, THANK YOU. I THINK I'LL STICK WI BEEF.
BEADS

The next day, Mr. Hogwash and the Critter Kids drove to the edge of the desert. On the way, they stopped at Joe's Trading Post. Everyone except LC went inside.

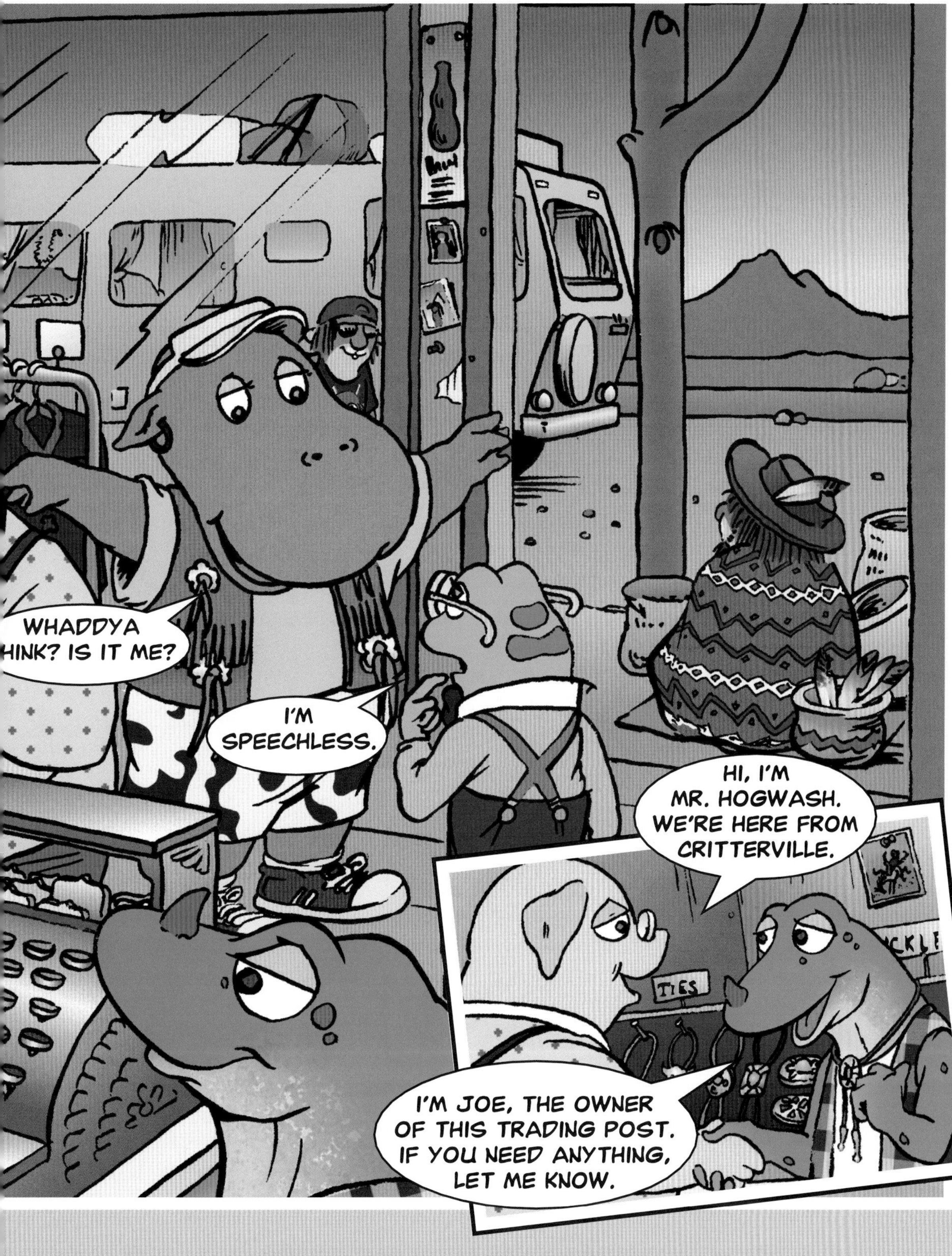
WHADDYA
HINK? IS IT ME?
I'M
SPEECHLESS.
HI, I'M
MR. HOGWASH.
WE'RE HERE FROM
CRITTERVILLE.
TIES
I'M JOE, THE OWNER
OF THIS TRADING POST.
IF YOU NEED ANYTHING,
LET ME KNOW.

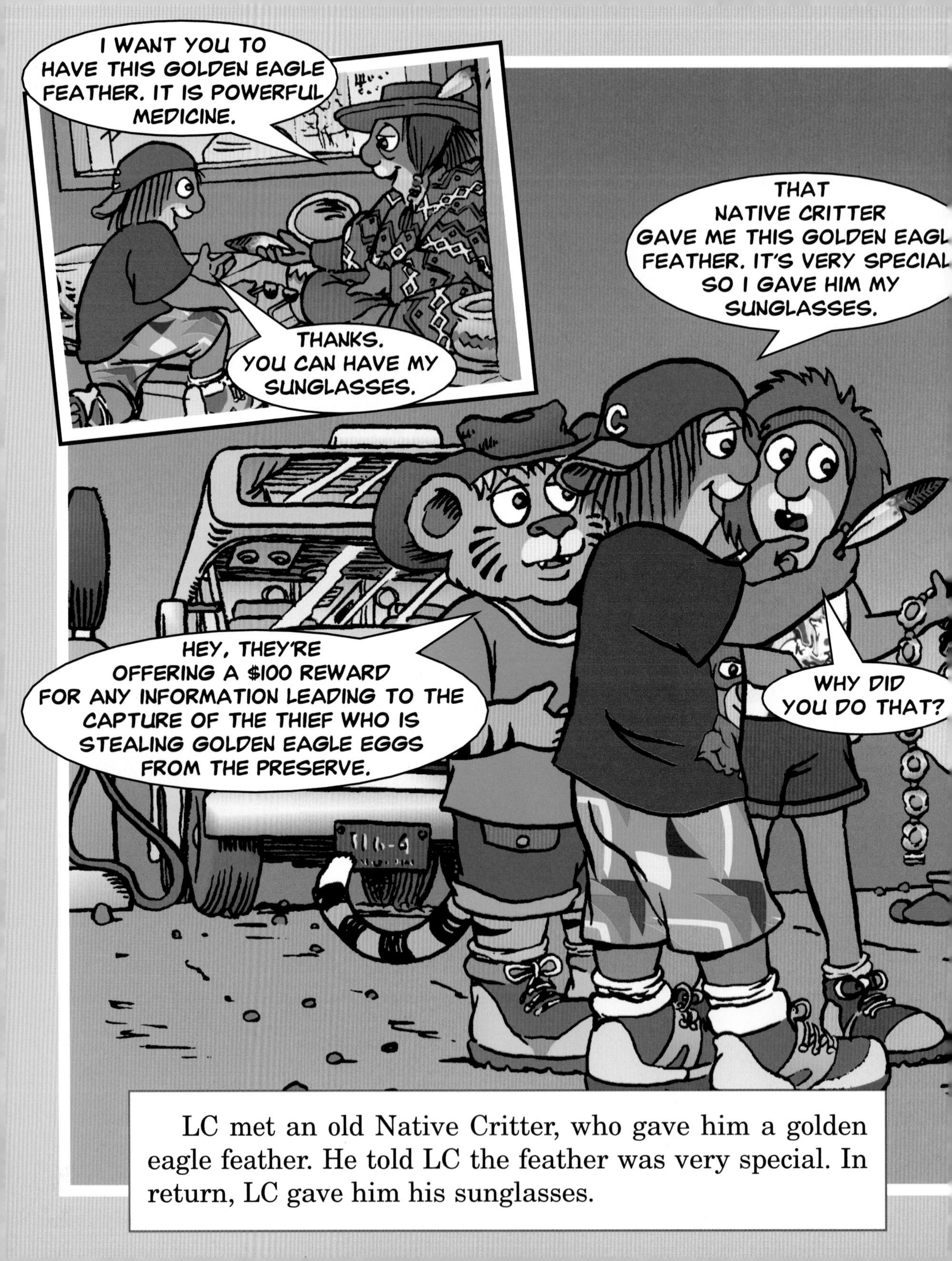
I WANT YOU TO HAVE THIS GOLDEN EAGLE FEATHER. IT IS POWERFUL MEDICINE.
THANKS. YOU CAN HAVE MY SUNGLASSES.
THAT NATIVE CRITTER GAVE ME THIS GOLDEN EAGL FEATHER. IT'S VERY SPECIAL SO I GAVE HIM MY SUNGLASSES.
WHY DID YOU DO THAT?
HEY, THEY'RE OFFERING A $100 REWARD FOR ANY INFORMATION LEADING TO THE CAPTURE OF THE THIEF WHO IS STEALING GOLDEN EAGLE EGGS FROM THE PRESERVE.

LC met an old Native Critter, who gave him a golden eagle feather. He told LC the feather was very special. In return, LC gave him his sunglasses.

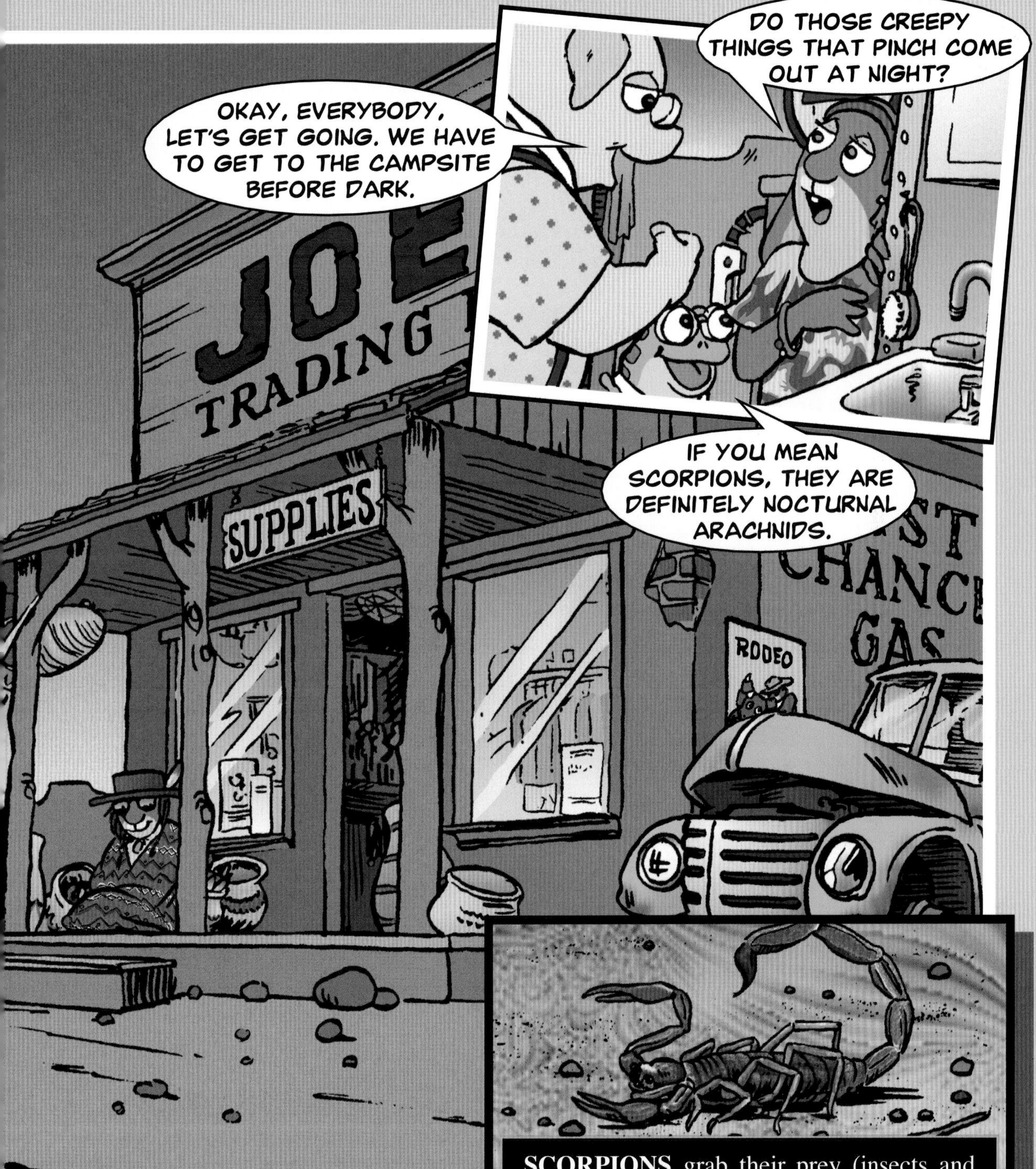
OKAY, EVERYBODY, LET'S GET GOING. WE HAVE TO GET TO THE CAMPSITE BEFORE DARK.
DO THOSE CREEPY THINGS THAT PINCH COME OUT AT NIGHT?
IF YOU MEAN SCORPIONS, THEY ARE DEFINITELY NOCTURNAL ARACHNIDS.
JOE
TRADING
SUPPLIES
CHANCE
GAS
RODEO

SCORPIONS grab their prey (insects and spiders) in their claws, crush them, and suck them dry. The sting of the most dangerous species can cause death to humans beings.

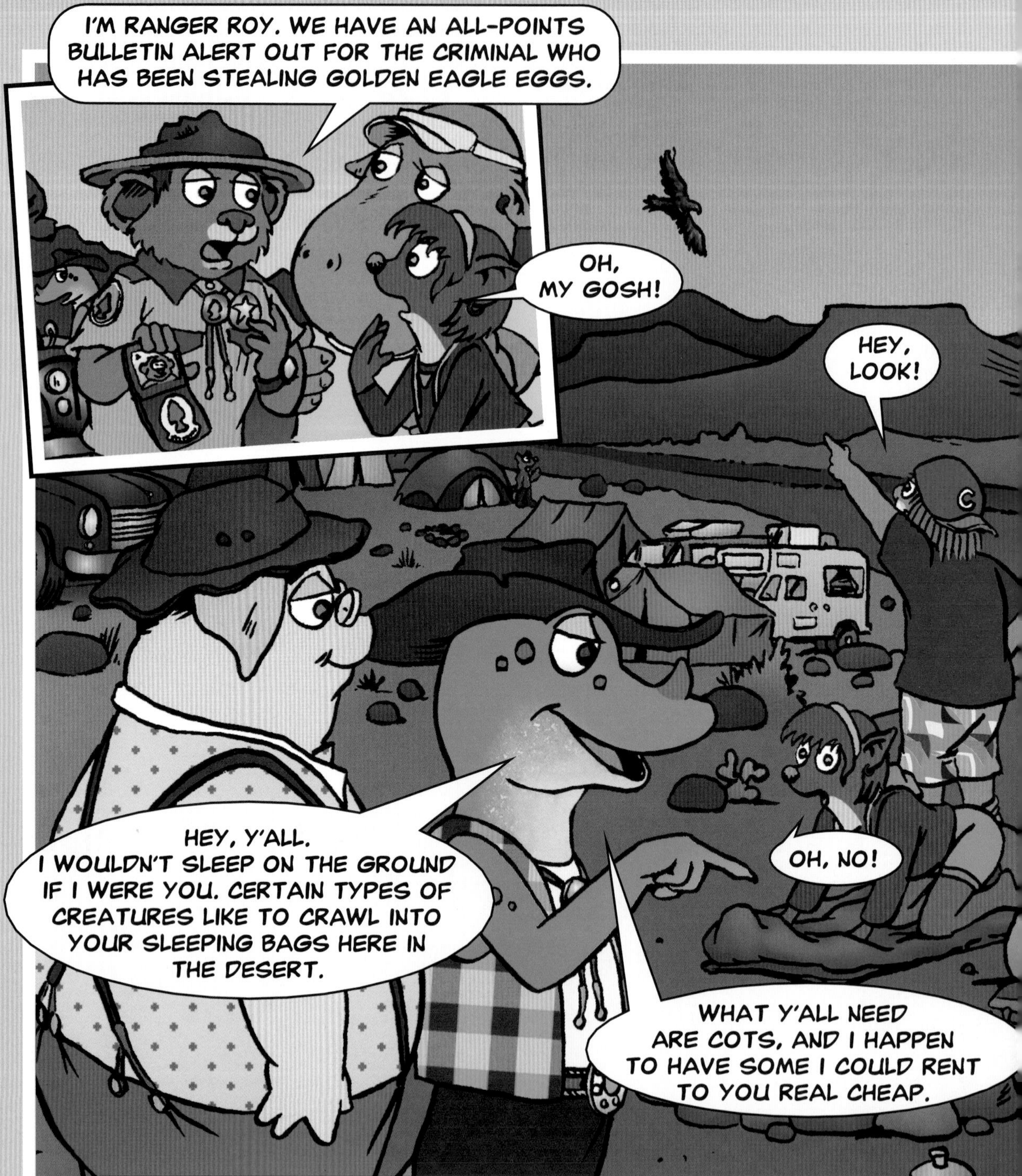
I'M RANGER ROY. WE HAVE AN ALL-POINTS BULLETIN ALERT OUT FOR THE CRIMINAL WHO HAS BEEN STEALING GOLDEN EAGLE EGGS.
OH, MY GOSH!
HEY, LOOK!
OH, NO!
HEY, Y'ALL. I WOULDN'T SLEEP ON THE GROUND IF I WERE YOU. CERTAIN TYPES OF CREATURES LIKE TO CRAWL INTO YOUR SLEEPING BAGS HERE IN THE DESERT.
WHAT Y'ALL NEED ARE COTS, AND I HAPPEN TO HAVE SOME I COULD RENT TO YOU REAL CHEAP.

When Mr. Hogwash and the Critter Kids got to the preserve, Joe helped them set up their campsite. Ranger Roy, the wildlife officer, told everyone that somebody was stealing golden eagle eggs from the preserve.

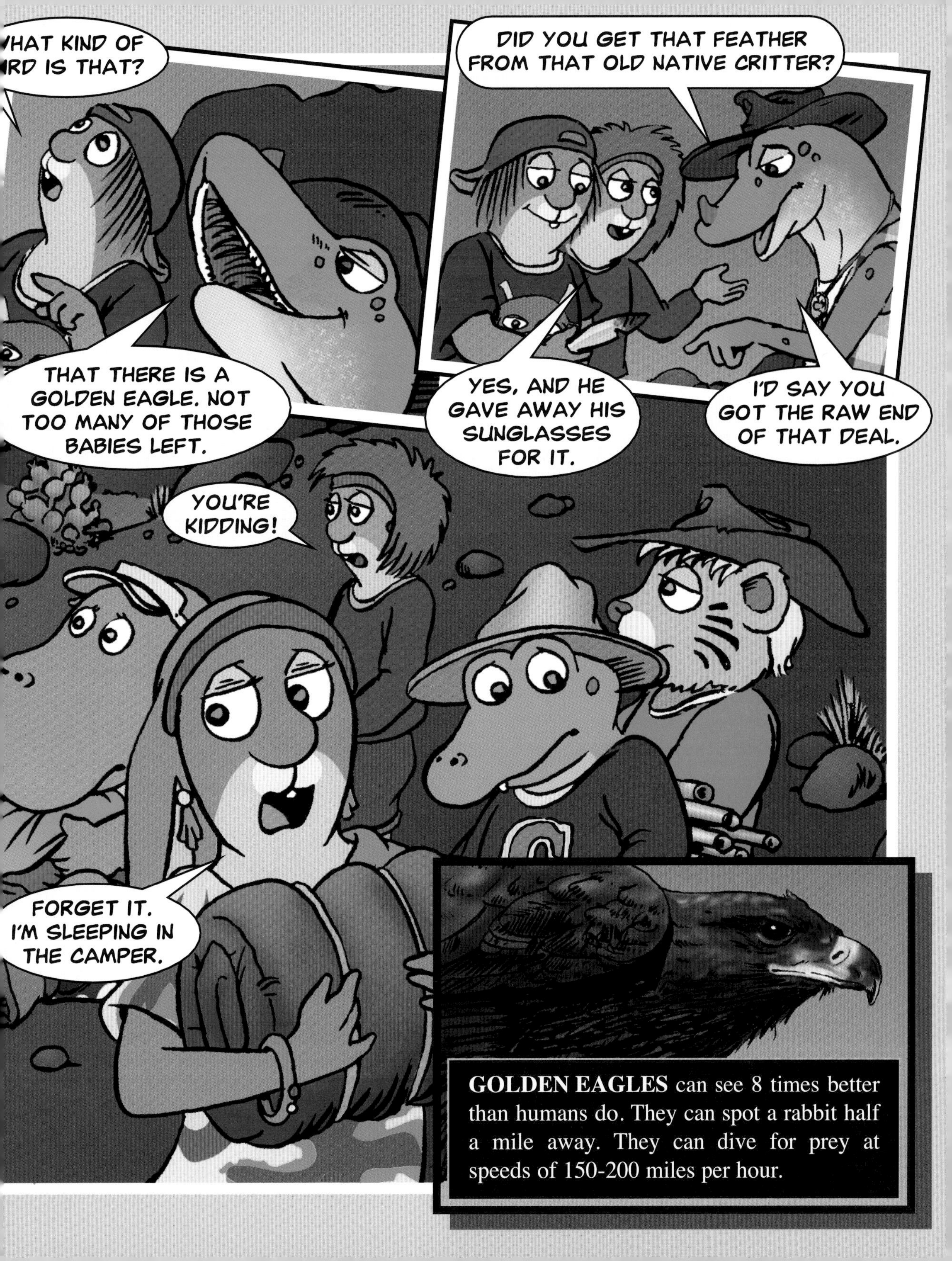

HAT KIND OF RD IS THAT?
THAT THERE IS A GOLDEN EAGLE. NOT TOO MANY OF THOSE BABIES LEFT.
DID YOU GET THAT FEATHER FROM THAT OLD NATIVE CRITTER?
YES, AND HE GAVE AWAY HIS SUNGLASSES FOR IT.
I'D SAY YOU GOT THE RAW END OF THAT DEAL.
YOU'RE KIDDING!
FORGET IT. I'M SLEEPING IN THE CAMPER.
GOLDEN EAGLES can see 8 times better than humans do. They can spot a rabbit half a mile away. They can dive for prey at speeds of 150-200 miles per hour.

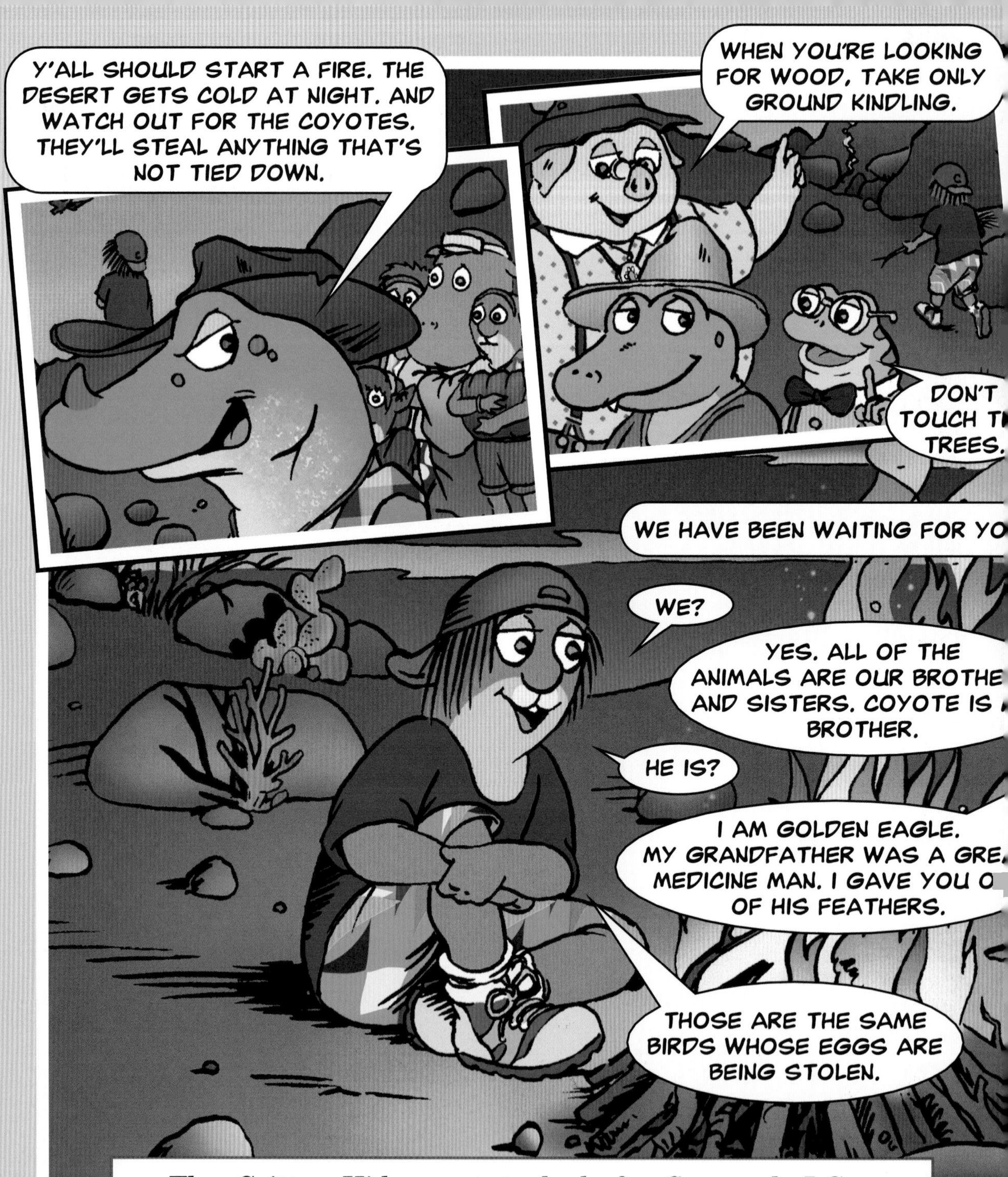
Y'ALL SHOULD START A FIRE. THE DESERT GETS COLD AT NIGHT. AND WATCH OUT FOR THE COYOTES. THEY'LL STEAL ANYTHING THAT'S NOT TIED DOWN.
WHEN YOU'RE LOOKING FOR WOOD, TAKE ONLY GROUND KINDLING.
DON'T TOUCH T
TREES.
WE HAVE BEEN WAITING FOR YO
WE?
YES. ALL OF THE ANIMALS ARE OUR BROTHE AND SISTERS. COYOTE IS BROTHER.
HE IS?
I AM GOLDEN EAGLE. MY GRANDFATHER WAS A GRE MEDICINE MAN. I GAVE YOU O OF HIS FEATHERS.
THOSE ARE THE SAME BIRDS WHOSE EGGS ARE BEING STOLEN.

The Critter Kids went to look for firewood. LC saw smoke and found the old Native Critter sitting in front of a big fire. He said his name was Golden Eagle and told LC to beware of the weasel.

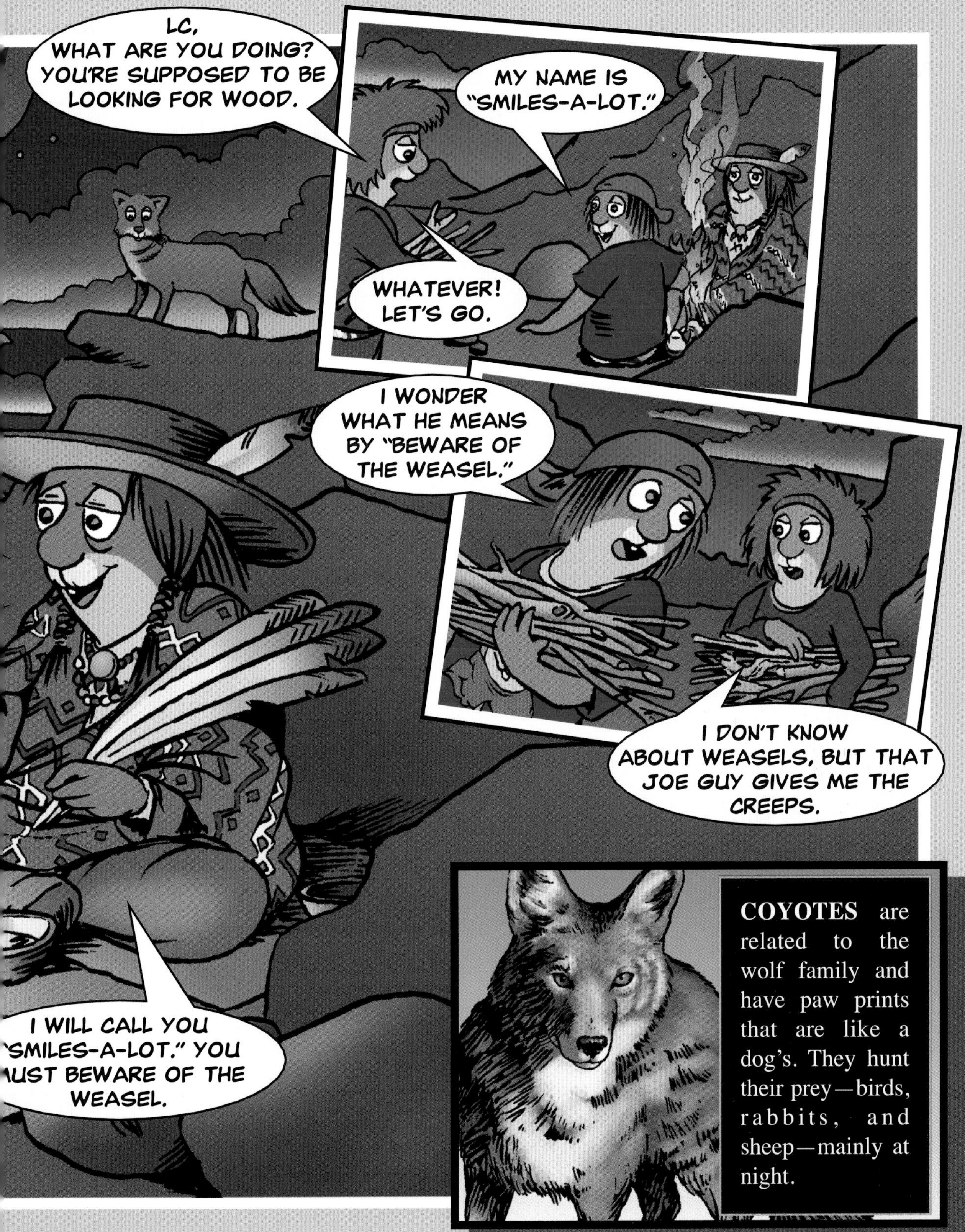
I WILL CALL YOU "SMILES-A-LOT." YOU UST BEWARE OF THE WEASEL.
LC, WHAT ARE YOU DOING? YOU'RE SUPPOSED TO BE LOOKING FOR WOOD.
MY NAME IS "SMILES-A-LOT."
WHATEVER! LET'S GO.
I WONDER WHAT HE MEANS BY "BEWARE OF THE WEASEL."
I DON'T KNOW ABOUT WEASELS, BUT THAT JOE GUY GIVES ME THE CREEPS.

COYOTES are related to the wolf family and have paw prints that are like a dog's. They hunt their prey—birds, rabbits, and sheep—mainly at night.

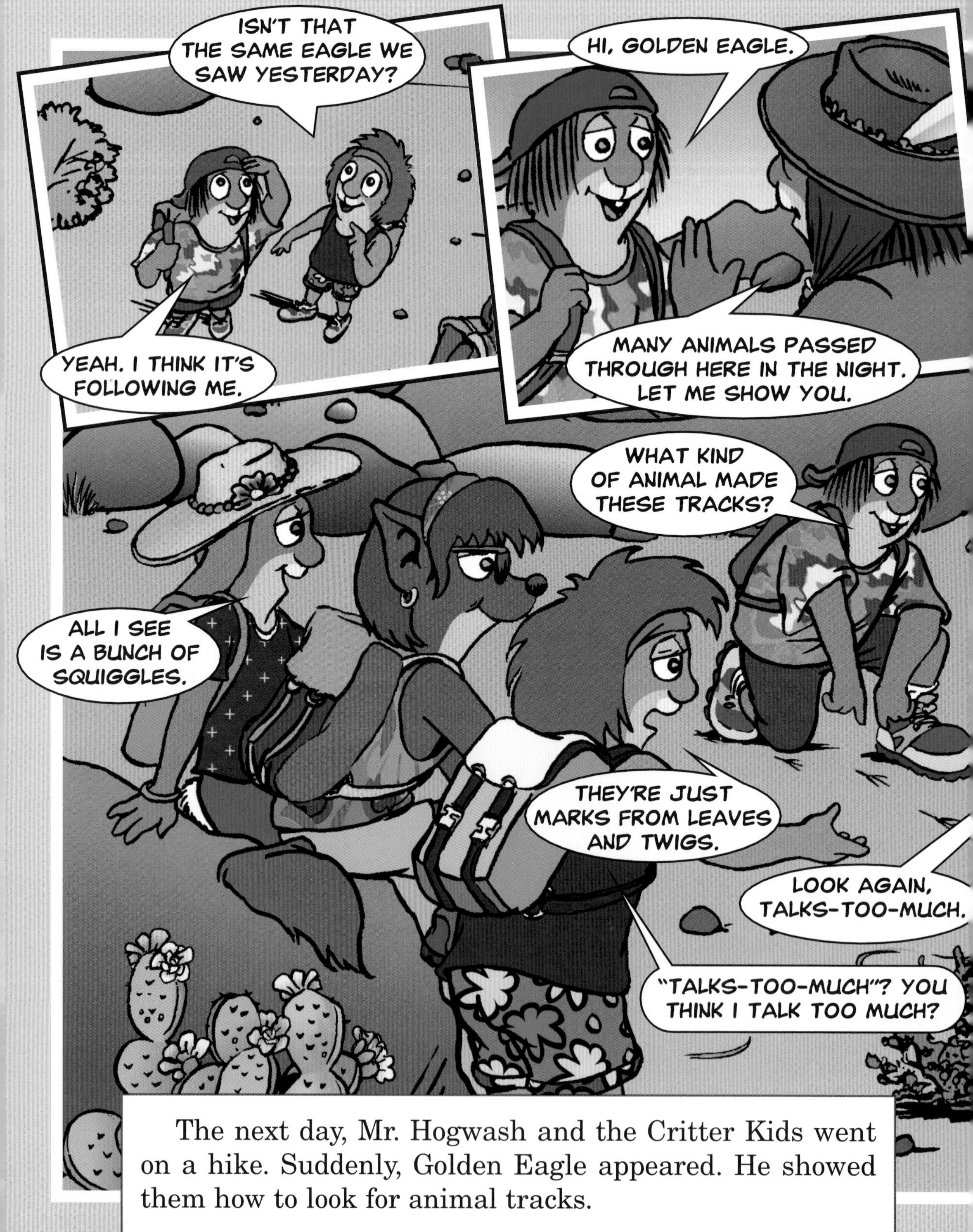
ISN'T THAT THE SAME EAGLE WE SAW YESTERDAY?
YEAH. I THINK IT'S FOLLOWING ME.
HI, GOLDEN EAGLE.
MANY ANIMALS PASSED THROUGH HERE IN THE NIGHT. LET ME SHOW YOU.
WHAT KIND OF ANIMAL MADE THESE TRACKS?
ALL I SEE IS A BUNCH OF SQUIGGLES.
THEY'RE JUST MARKS FROM LEAVES AND TWIGS.
LOOK AGAIN, TALKS-TOO-MUCH.
"TALKS-TOO-MUCH"? YOU THINK I TALK TOO MUCH?

The next day, Mr. Hogwash and the Critter Kids went on a hike. Suddenly, Golden Eagle appeared. He showed them how to look for animal tracks.

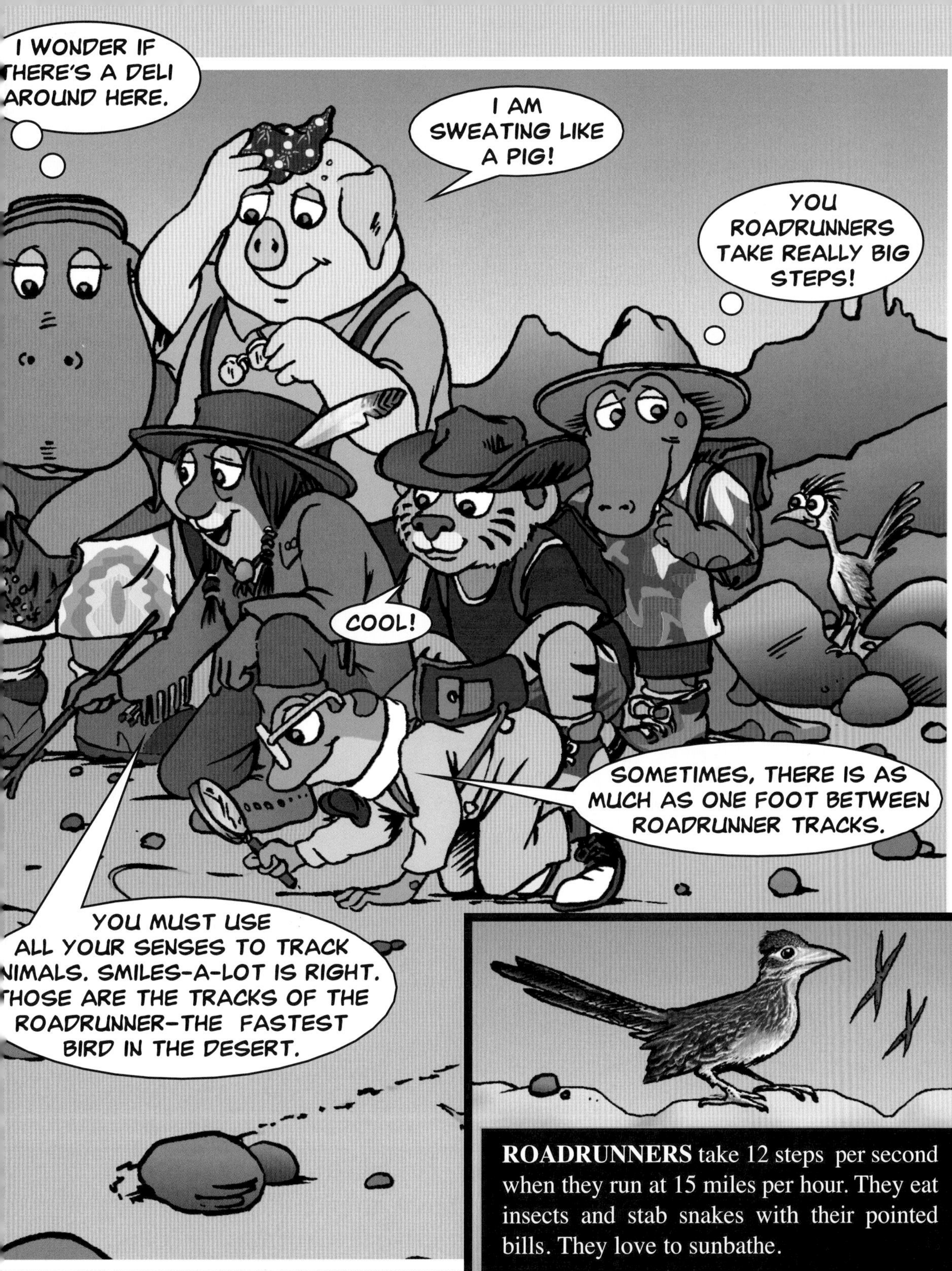

I WONDER IF HERE'S A DELI AROUND HERE.
I AM SWEATING LIKE A PIG!
YOU ROADRUNNERS TAKE REALLY BIG STEPS!
COOL!
SOMETIMES, THERE IS AS MUCH AS ONE FOOT BETWEEN ROADRUNNER TRACKS.
YOU MUST USE ALL YOUR SENSES TO TRACK NIMALS. SMILES-A-LOT IS RIGHT. HOSE ARE THE TRACKS OF THE ROADRUNNER–THE FASTEST BIRD IN THE DESERT.

ROADRUNNERS take 12 steps per second when they run at 15 miles per hour. They eat insects and stab snakes with their pointed bills. They love to sunbathe.

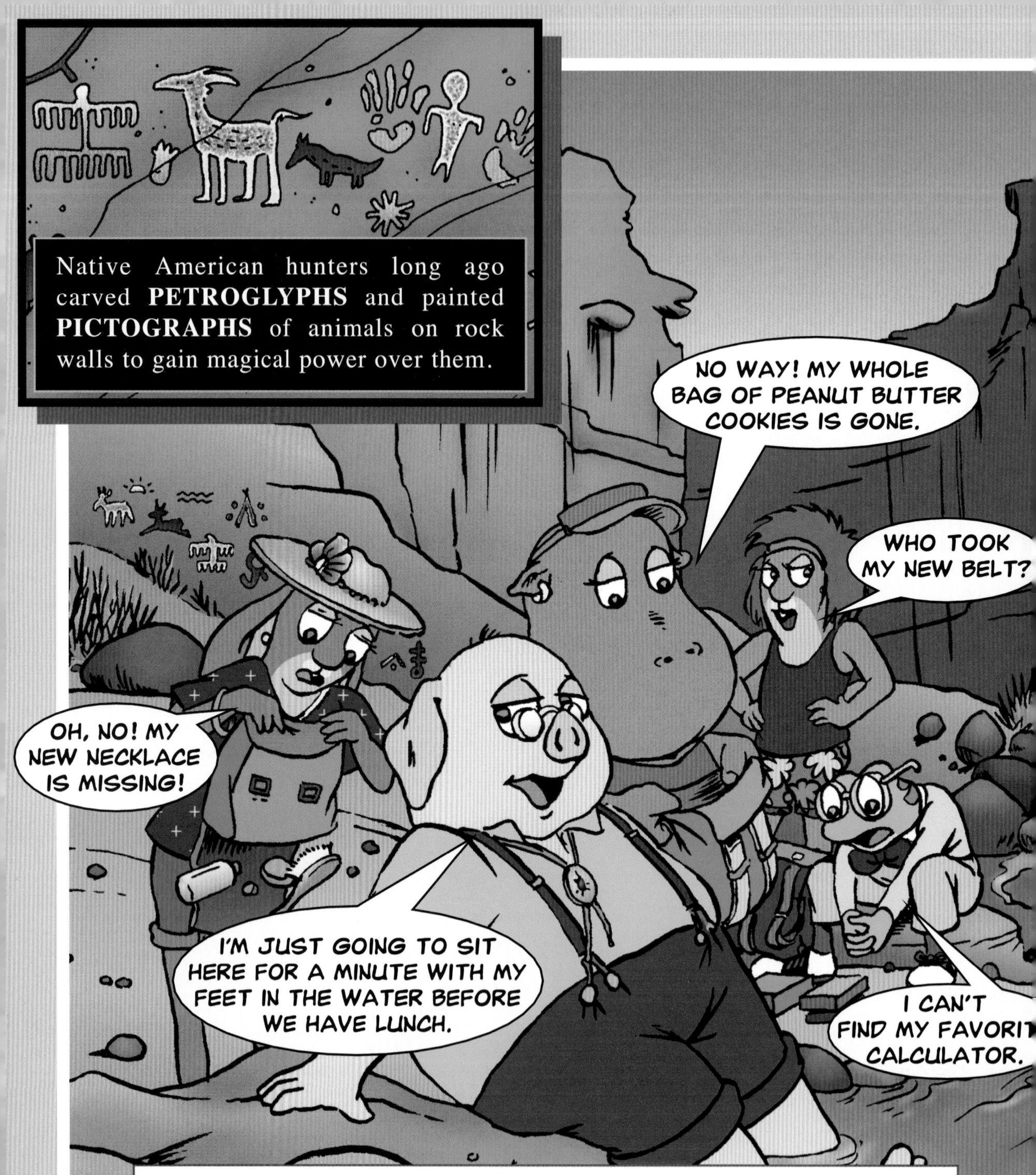
NO WAY! MY WHOLE BAG OF PEANUT BUTTER COOKIES IS GONE.
WHO TOOK MY NEW BELT?
OH, NO! MY NEW NECKLACE IS MISSING!
I'M JUST GOING TO SIT HERE FOR A MINUTE WITH MY FEET IN THE WATER BEFORE WE HAVE LUNCH.
I CAN'T FIND MY FAVORIT CALCULATOR.

Native American hunters long ago carved **PETROGLYPHS** and painted **PICTOGRAPHS** of animals on rock walls to gain magical power over them.

After Golden Eagle left, Mr. Hogwash and the Critter Kids stopped at an oasis to have a picnic. When they unpacked, they discovered lots of their stuff was missing. Joe told them the coyotes had probably stolen it.

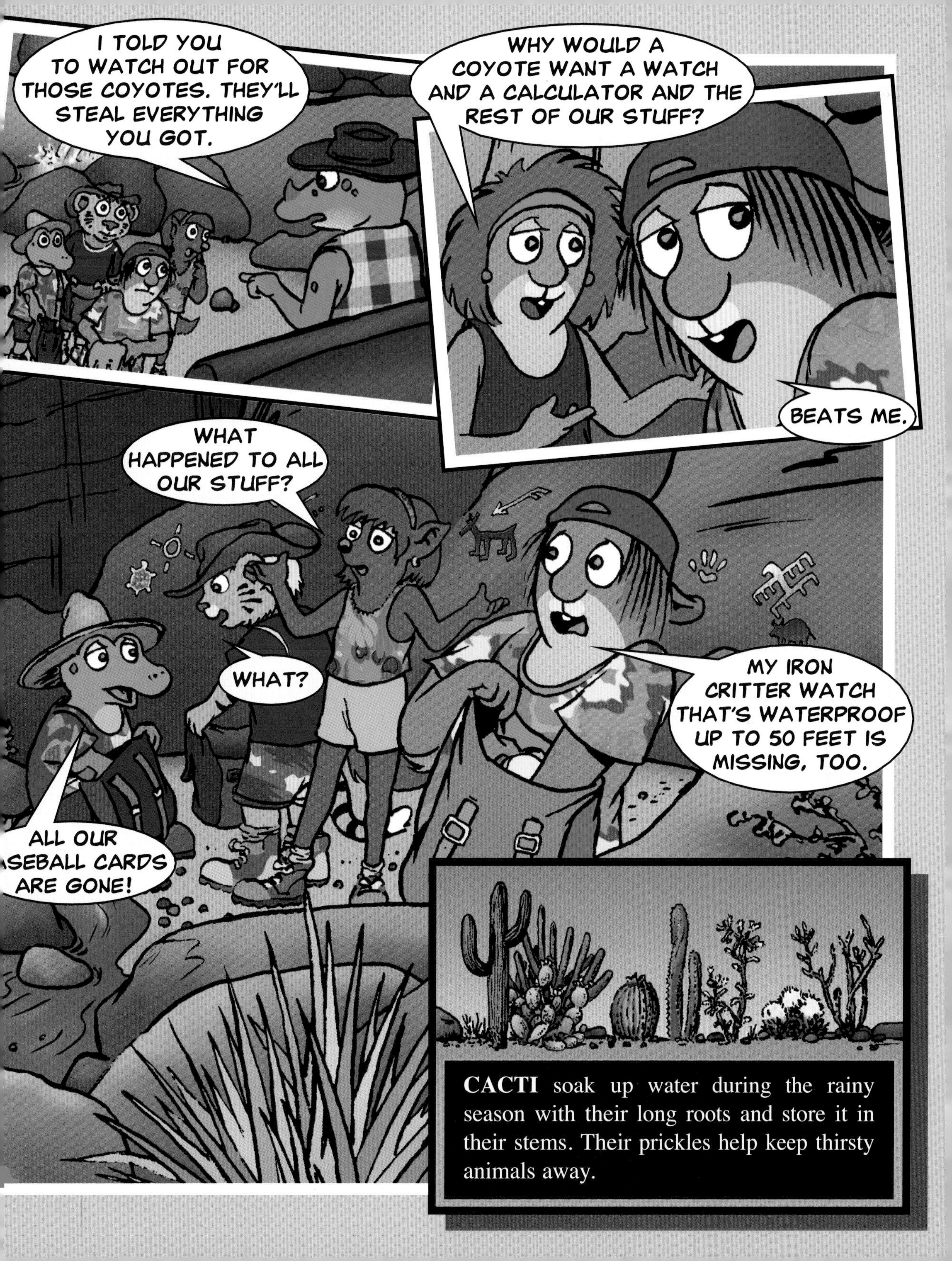
I TOLD YOU TO WATCH OUT FOR THOSE COYOTES. THEY'LL STEAL EVERYTHING YOU GOT.
WHY WOULD A COYOTE WANT A WATCH AND A CALCULATOR AND THE REST OF OUR STUFF?
BEATS ME.
WHAT HAPPENED TO ALL OUR STUFF?
WHAT?
MY IRON CRITTER WATCH THAT'S WATERPROOF UP TO 50 FEET IS MISSING, TOO.
ALL OUR SEBALL CARDS ARE GONE!

CACTI soak up water during the rainy season with their long roots and store it in their stems. Their prickles help keep thirsty animals away.

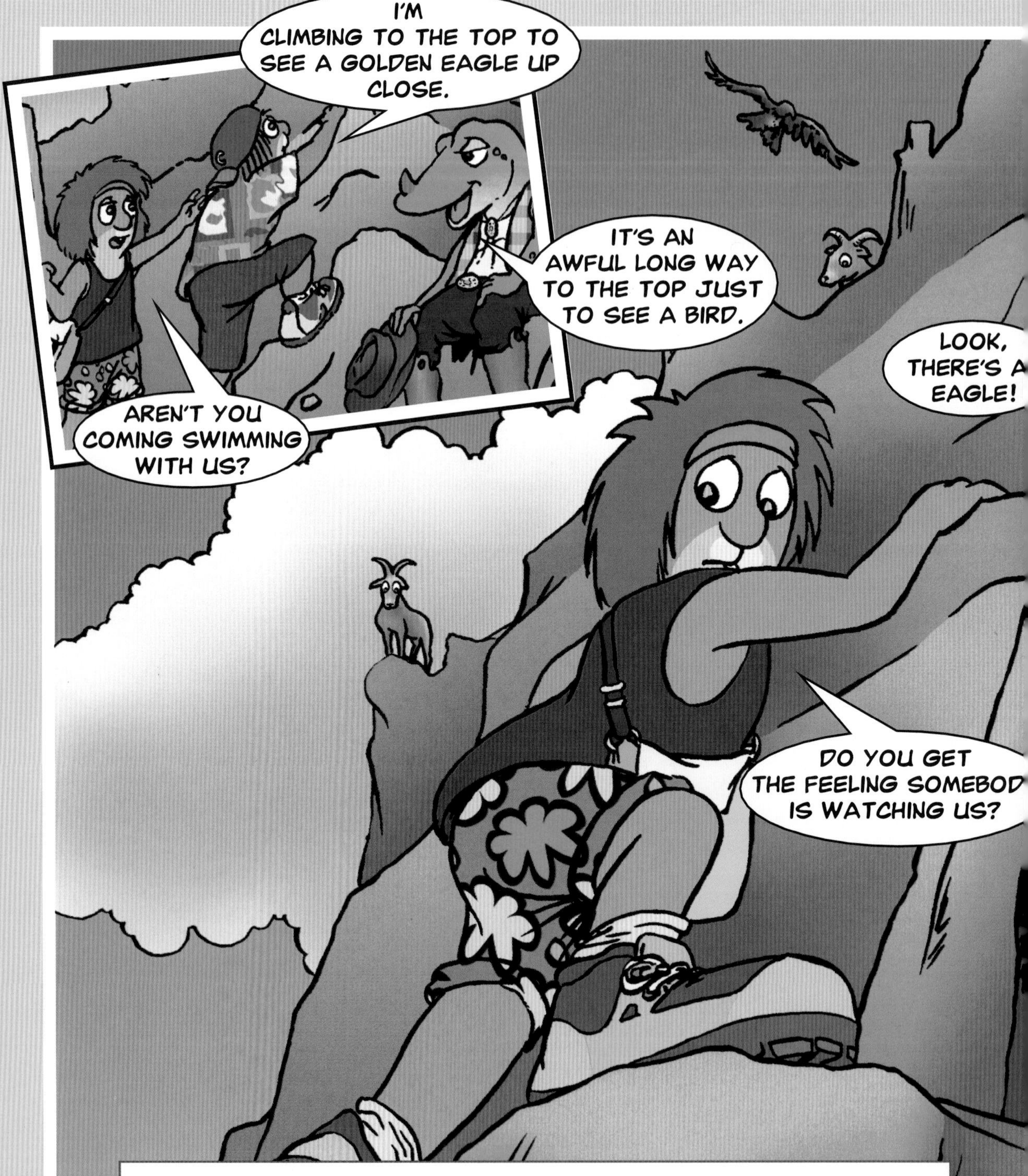
I'M CLIMBING TO THE TOP TO SEE A GOLDEN EAGLE UP CLOSE.
AREN'T YOU COMING SWIMMING WITH US?
IT'S AN AWFUL LONG WAY TO THE TOP JUST TO SEE A BIRD.
LOOK, THERE'S A EAGLE!
DO YOU GET THE FEELING SOMEBOD IS WATCHING US?

After lunch, the Kids wanted to go swimming, but LC just had to see a golden eagle bird. He and Gabby decided to climb all the way to the top of the cliff.

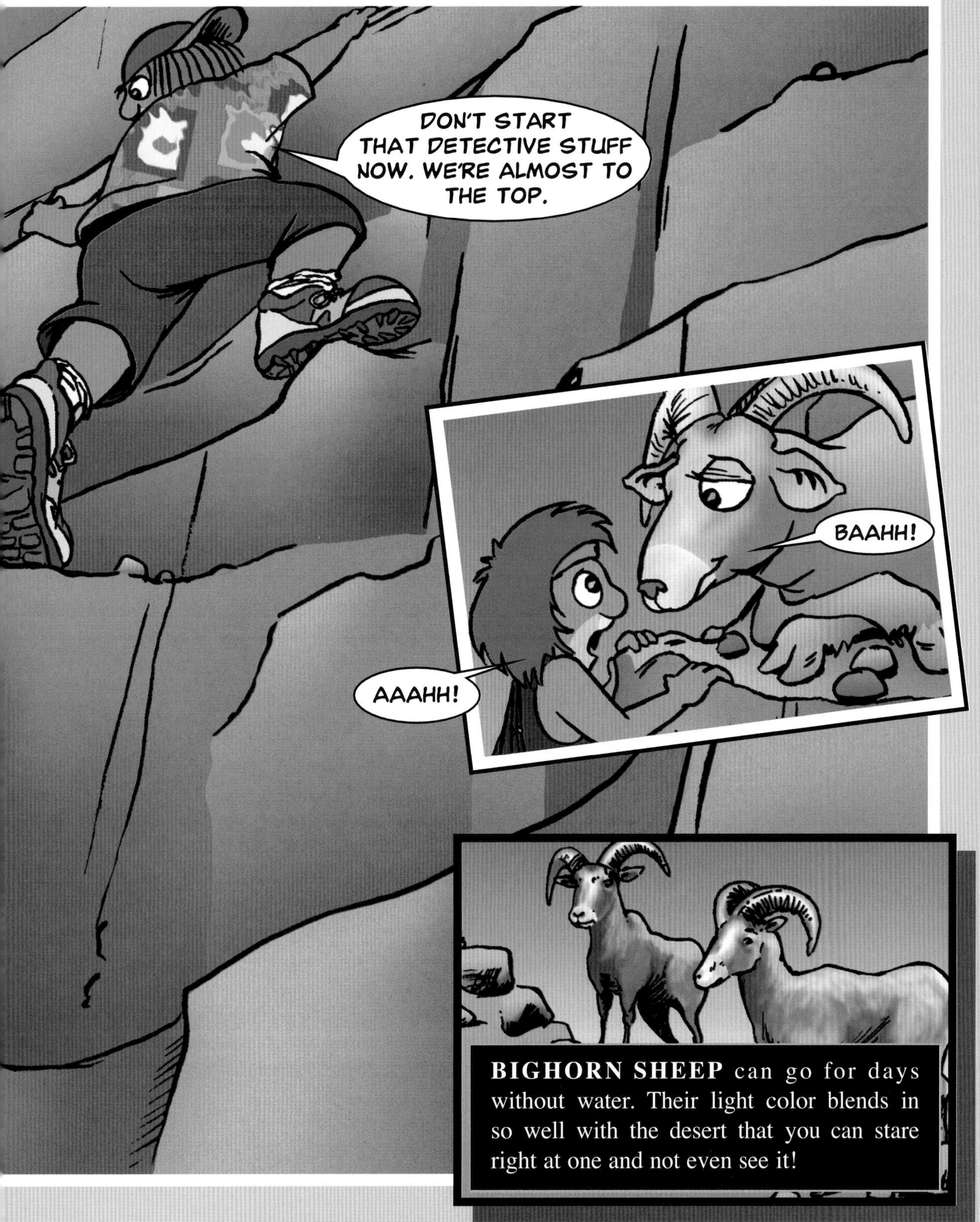
DON'T START THAT DETECTIVE STUFF NOW. WE'RE ALMOST TO THE TOP.
BAAHH!
AAAHH!
BIGHORN SHEEP can go for days without water. Their light color blends in so well with the desert that you can stare right at one and not even see it!

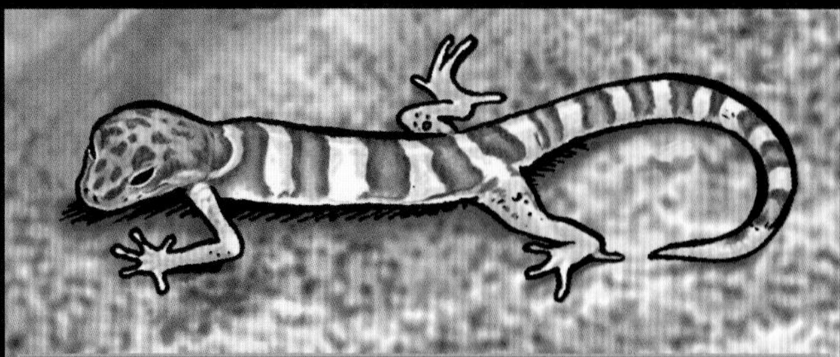

GECKO LIZARDS will shed their tails or part of their skin if attacked. When shed, the tail will wiggle for a few minutes to confuse the attacker so the lizard can escape.

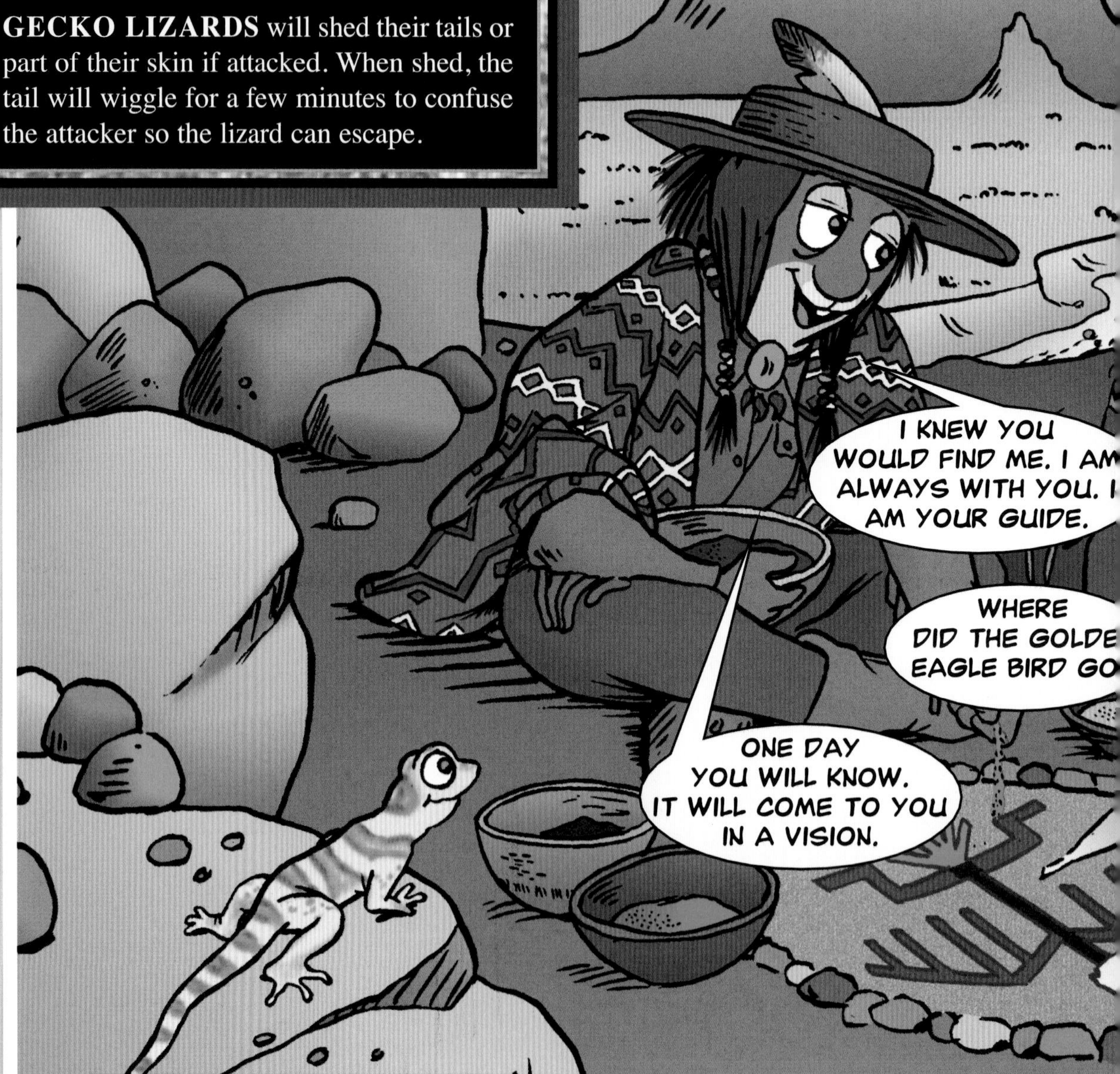
I KNEW YOU WOULD FIND ME. I AM ALWAYS WITH YOU. I AM YOUR GUIDE.
WHERE DID THE GOLDE EAGLE BIRD GO
ONE DAY YOU WILL KNOW. IT WILL COME TO YOU IN A VISION.

At the top of the cliff, LC found Golden Eagle. There were no golden eagle birds anywhere, only an empty nest with strange boot prints around it.

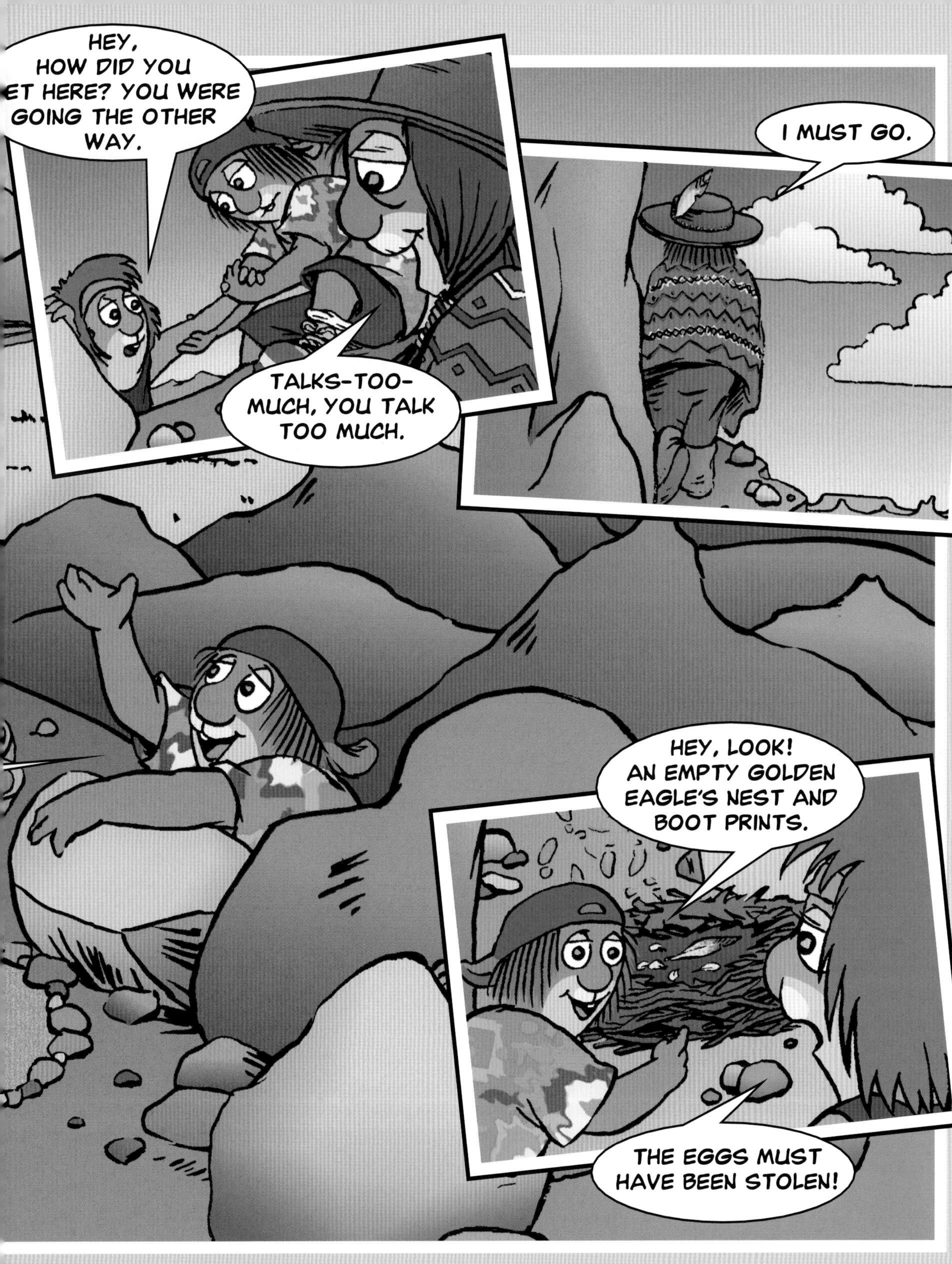

HEY, HOW DID YOU ET HERE? YOU WERE GOING THE OTHER WAY.
TALKS-TOO-MUCH, YOU TALK TOO MUCH.
I MUST GO.
HEY, LOOK! AN EMPTY GOLDEN EAGLE'S NEST AND BOOT PRINTS.
THE EGGS MUST HAVE BEEN STOLEN!

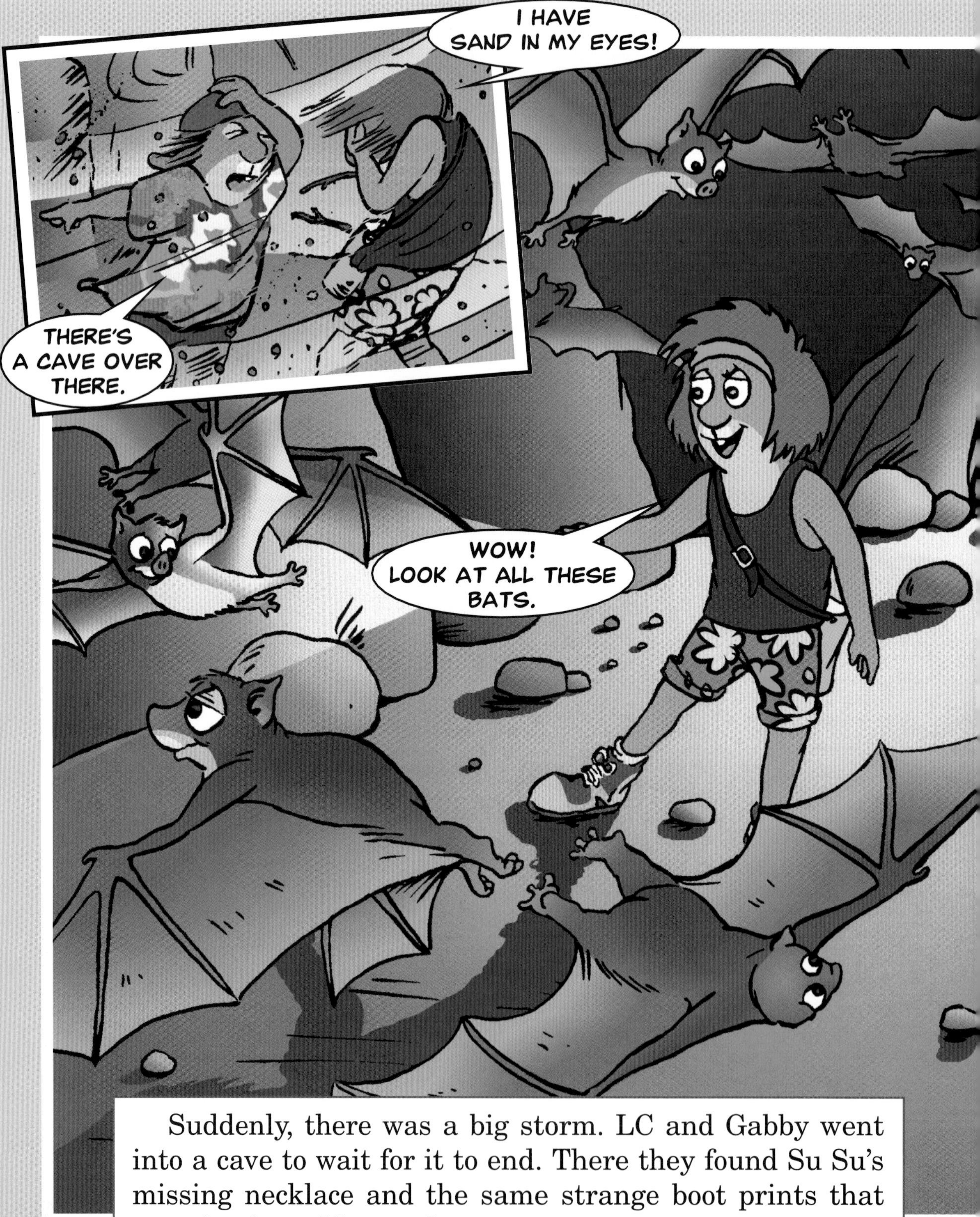
I HAVE SAND IN MY EYES!
THERE'S A CAVE OVER THERE.
WOW! LOOK AT ALL THESE BATS.

Suddenly, there was a big storm. LC and Gabby went into a cave to wait for it to end. There they found Su Su's missing necklace and the same strange boot prints that were by the golden eagle nest.

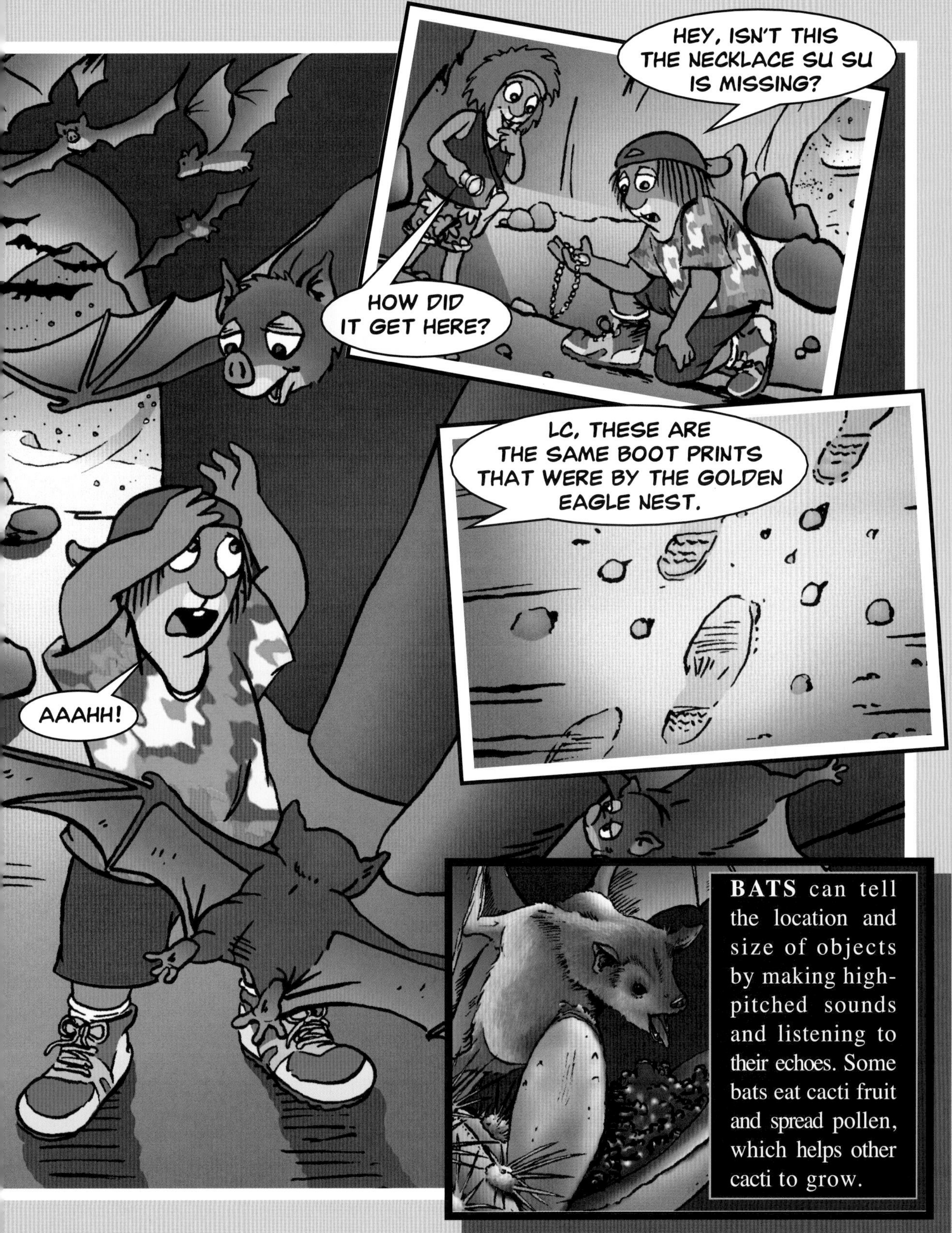
HEY, ISN'T THIS THE NECKLACE SU SU IS MISSING?
HOW DID IT GET HERE?
LC, THESE ARE THE SAME BOOT PRINTS THAT WERE BY THE GOLDEN EAGLE NEST.
AAAHH!

BATS can tell the location and size of objects by making high-pitched sounds and listening to their echoes. Some bats eat cacti fruit and spread pollen, which helps other cacti to grow.

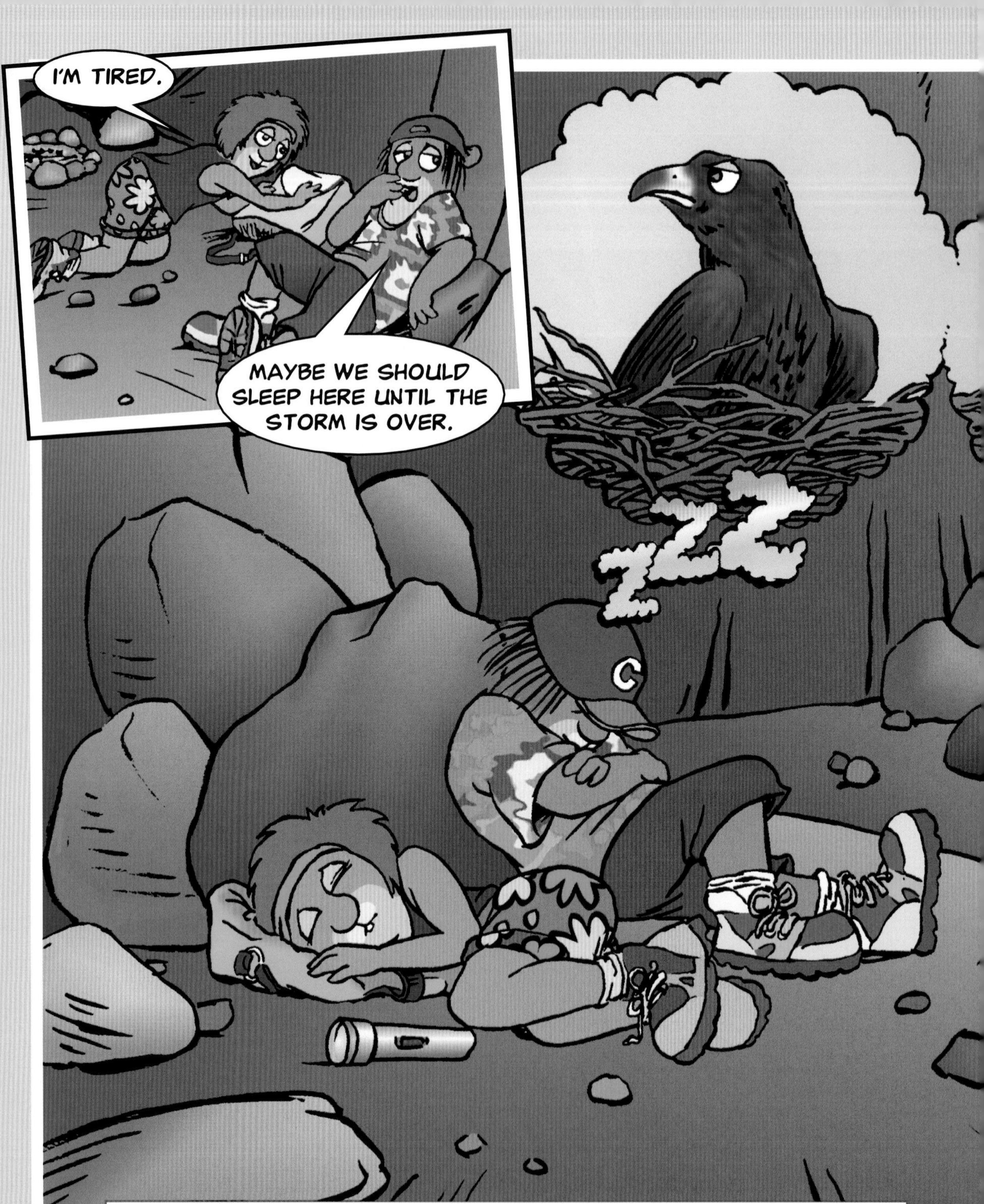
I'M TIRED.
MAYBE WE SHOULD SLEEP HERE UNTIL THE STORM IS OVER.
ZZZ

While the storm raged outside, both LC and Gabby fell into a deep sleep. LC had a strange dream.

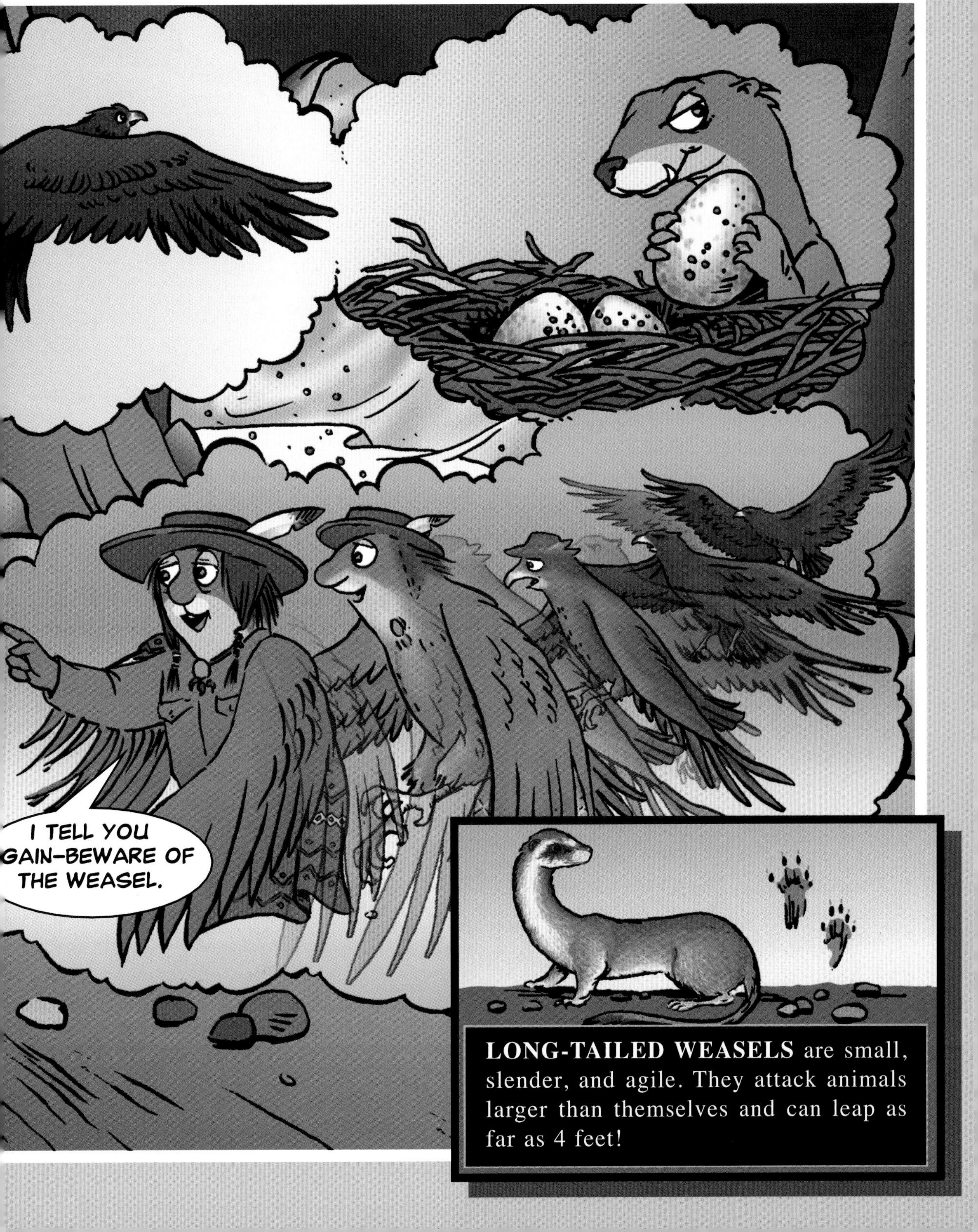
I TELL YOU GAIN–BEWARE OF THE WEASEL.

LONG-TAILED WEASELS are small, slender, and agile. They attack animals larger than themselves and can leap as far as 4 feet!

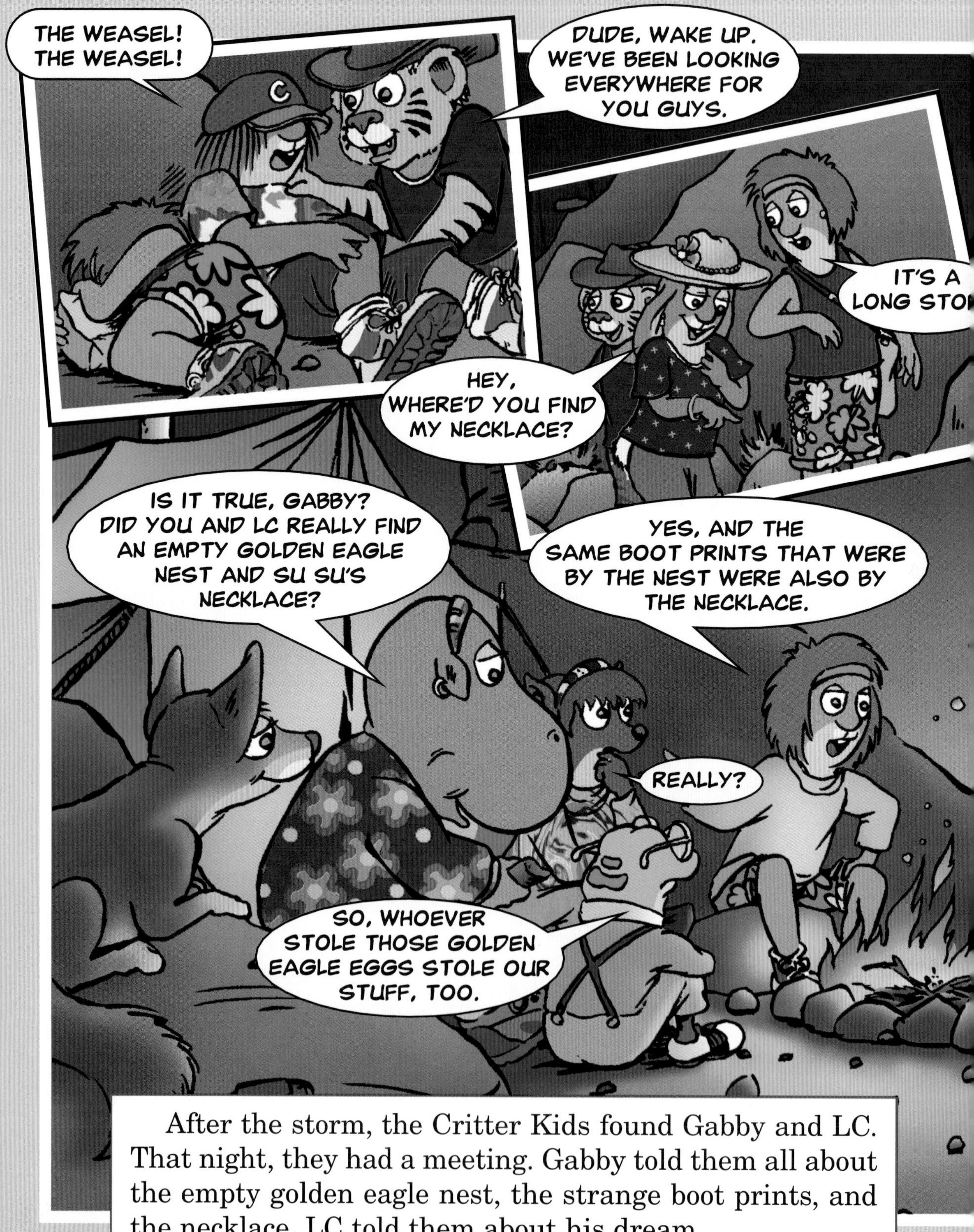
THE WEASEL! THE WEASEL!
DUDE, WAKE UP. WE'VE BEEN LOOKING EVERYWHERE FOR YOU GUYS.
IT'S A LONG STO
HEY, WHERE'D YOU FIND MY NECKLACE?
IS IT TRUE, GABBY? DID YOU AND LC REALLY FIND AN EMPTY GOLDEN EAGLE NEST AND SU SU'S NECKLACE?
YES, AND THE SAME BOOT PRINTS THAT WERE BY THE NEST WERE ALSO BY THE NECKLACE.
REALLY?
SO, WHOEVER STOLE THOSE GOLDEN EAGLE EGGS STOLE OUR STUFF, TOO.

After the storm, the Critter Kids found Gabby and LC. That night, they had a meeting. Gabby told them all about the empty golden eagle nest, the strange boot prints, and the necklace. LC told them about his dream.

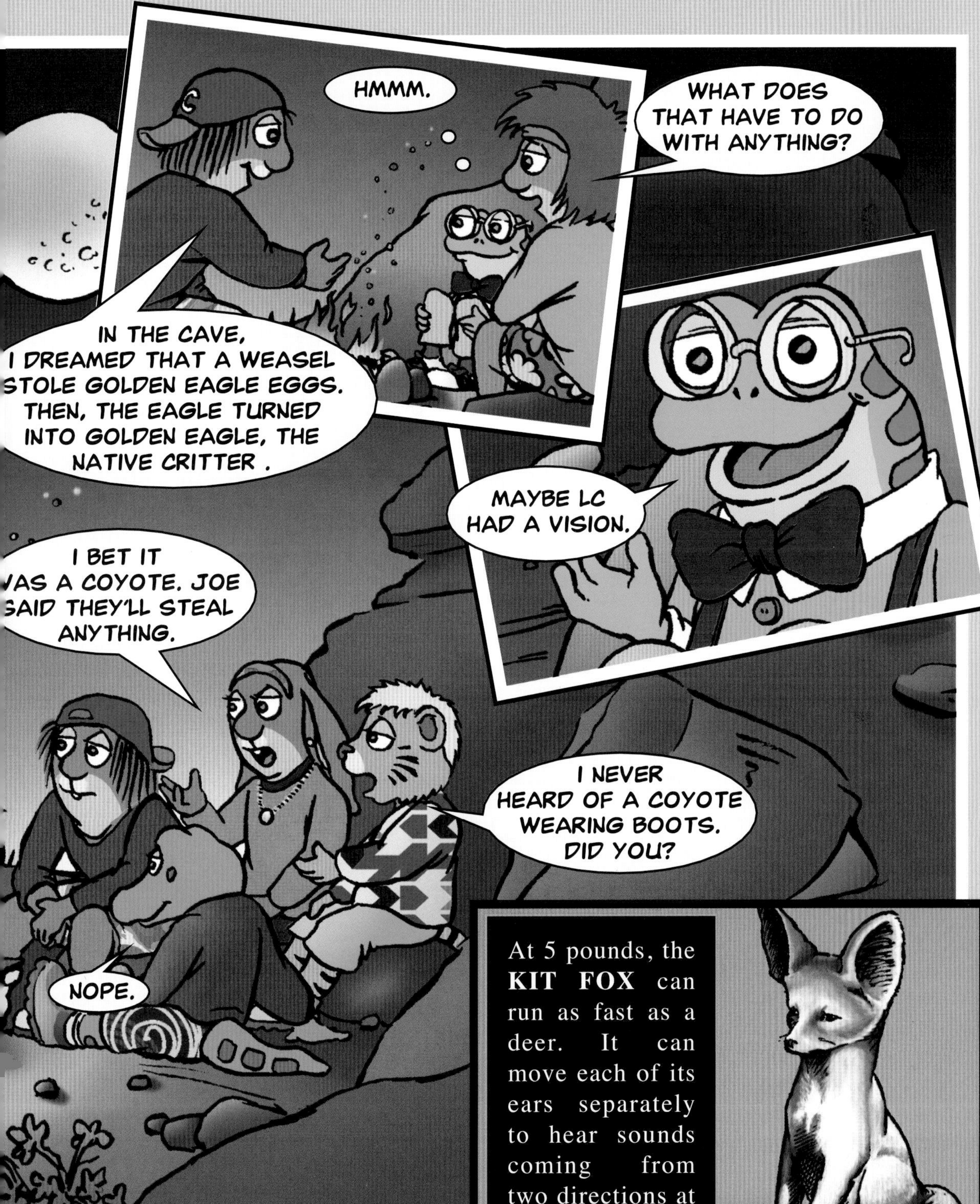
IN THE CAVE, I DREAMED THAT A WEASEL STOLE GOLDEN EAGLE EGGS. THEN, THE EAGLE TURNED INTO GOLDEN EAGLE, THE NATIVE CRITTER .
HMMM.
WHAT DOES THAT HAVE TO DO WITH ANYTHING?
MAYBE LC HAD A VISION.
I BET IT
AS A COYOTE. JOE
AID THEY'LL STEAL
ANYTHING.
I NEVER HEARD OF A COYOTE WEARING BOOTS. DID YOU?
NOPE.

At 5 pounds, the **KIT FOX** can run as fast as a deer. It can move each of its ears separately to hear sounds coming from two directions at the same time.

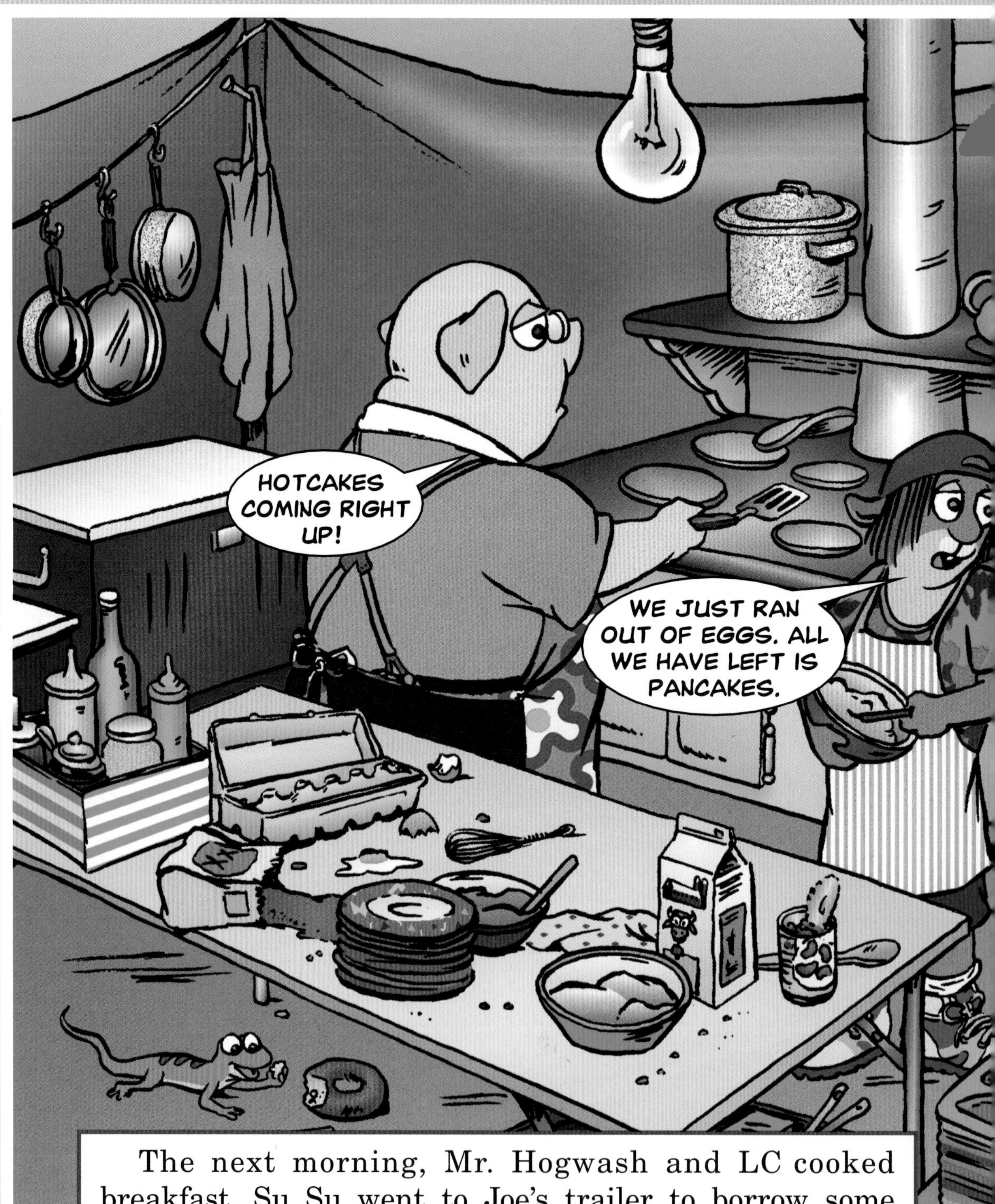
HOTCAKES COMING RIGHT UP!
WE JUST RAN OUT OF EGGS. ALL WE HAVE LEFT IS PANCAKES.

The next morning, Mr. Hogwash and LC cooked breakfast. Su Su went to Joe's trailer to borrow some eggs, but what she brought back were not regular eggs. They were golden eagle eggs!

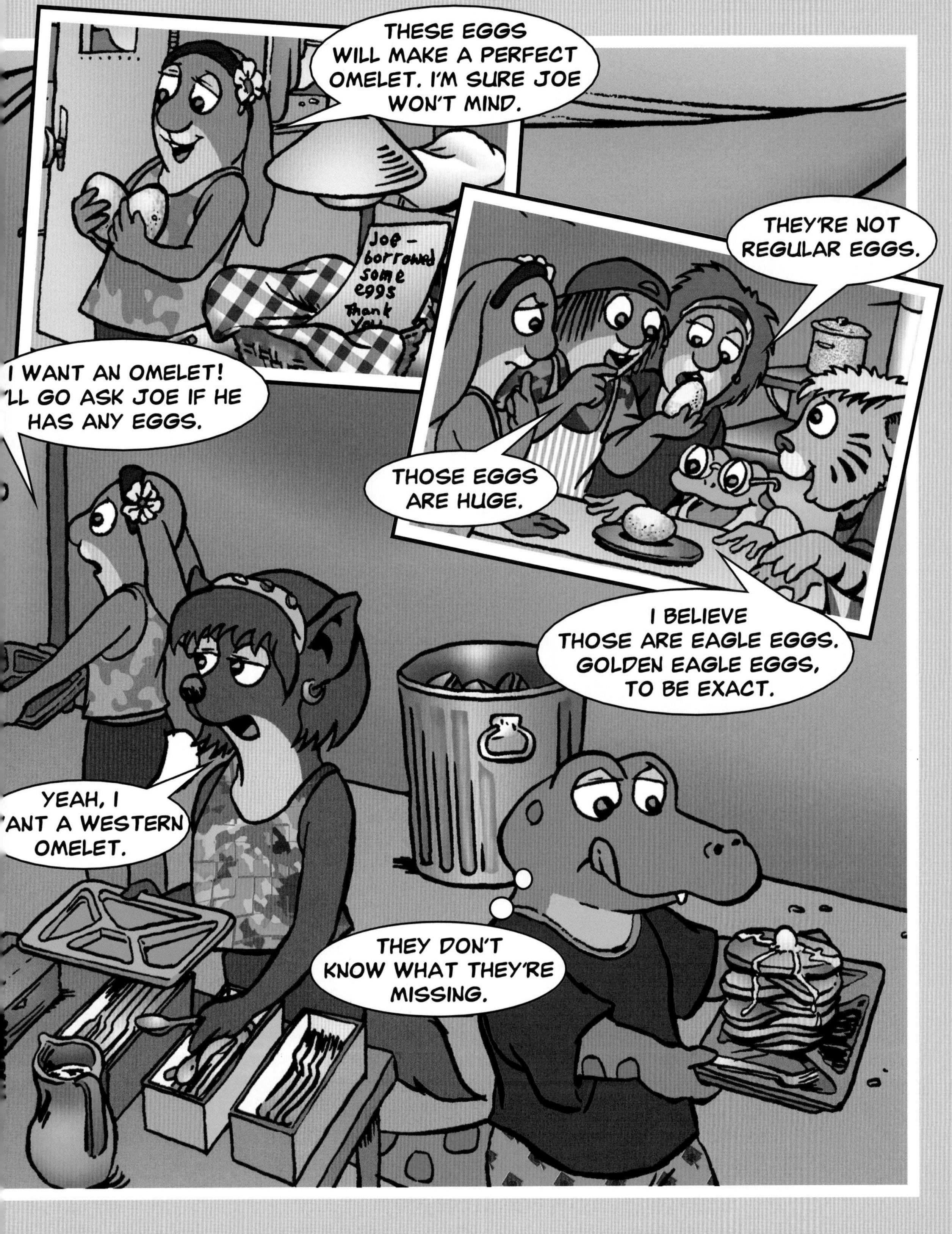
THESE EGGS WILL MAKE A PERFECT OMELET. I'M SURE JOE WON'T MIND.
Joe - borrowed some eggs Thank You
THEY'RE NOT REGULAR EGGS.
THOSE EGGS ARE HUGE.
I BELIEVE THOSE ARE EAGLE EGGS. GOLDEN EAGLE EGGS, TO BE EXACT.
I WANT AN OMELET! 'LL GO ASK JOE IF HE HAS ANY EGGS.
YEAH, I 'ANT A WESTERN OMELET.
THEY DON'T KNOW WHAT THEY'RE MISSING.

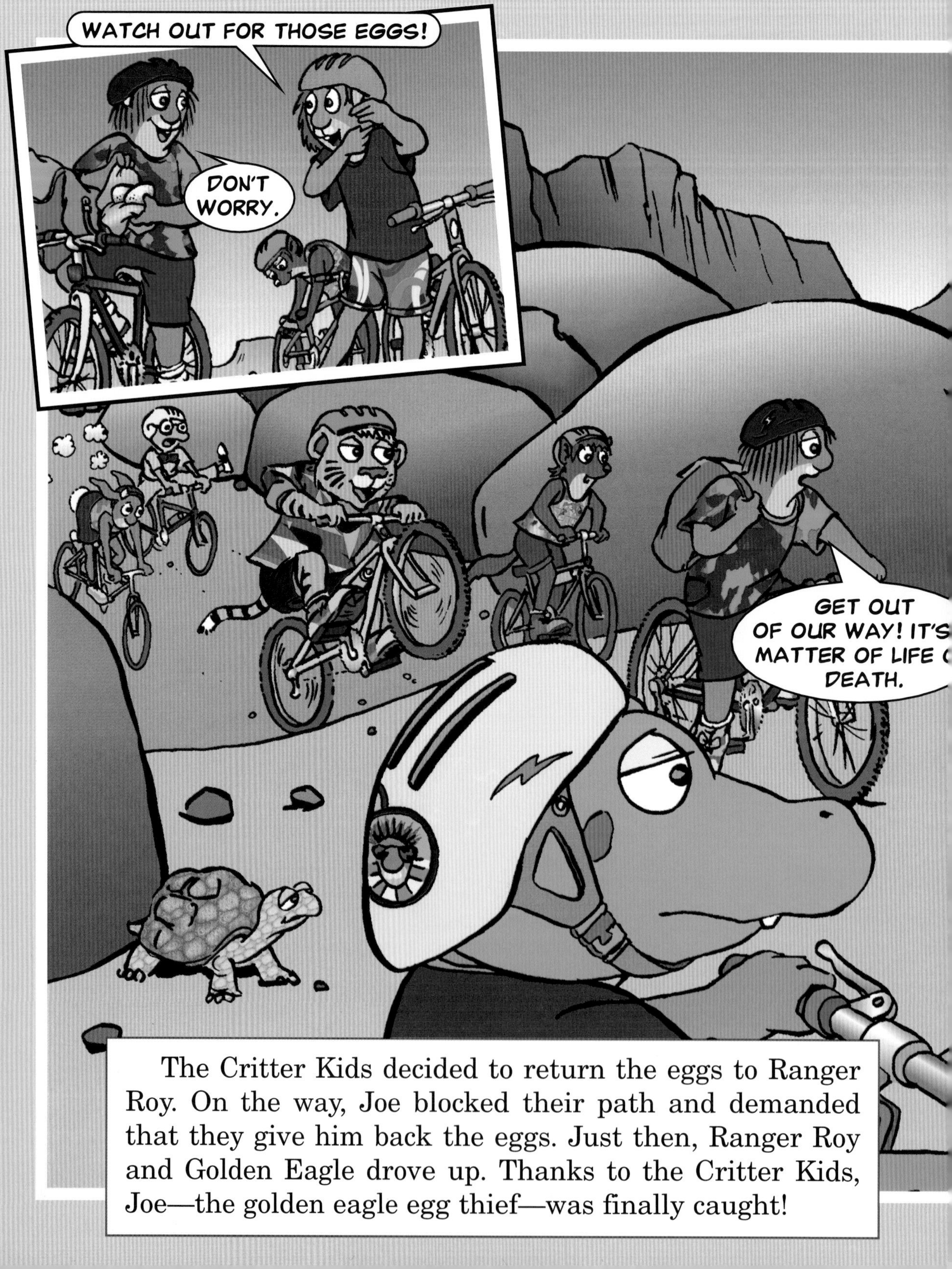
WATCH OUT FOR THOSE EGGS!
DON'T WORRY.
GET OUT OF OUR WAY! IT'S MATTER OF LIFE
DEATH.

The Critter Kids decided to return the eggs to Ranger Roy. On the way, Joe blocked their path and demanded that they give him back the eggs. Just then, Ranger Roy and Golden Eagle drove up. Thanks to the Critter Kids, Joe—the golden eagle egg thief—was finally caught!

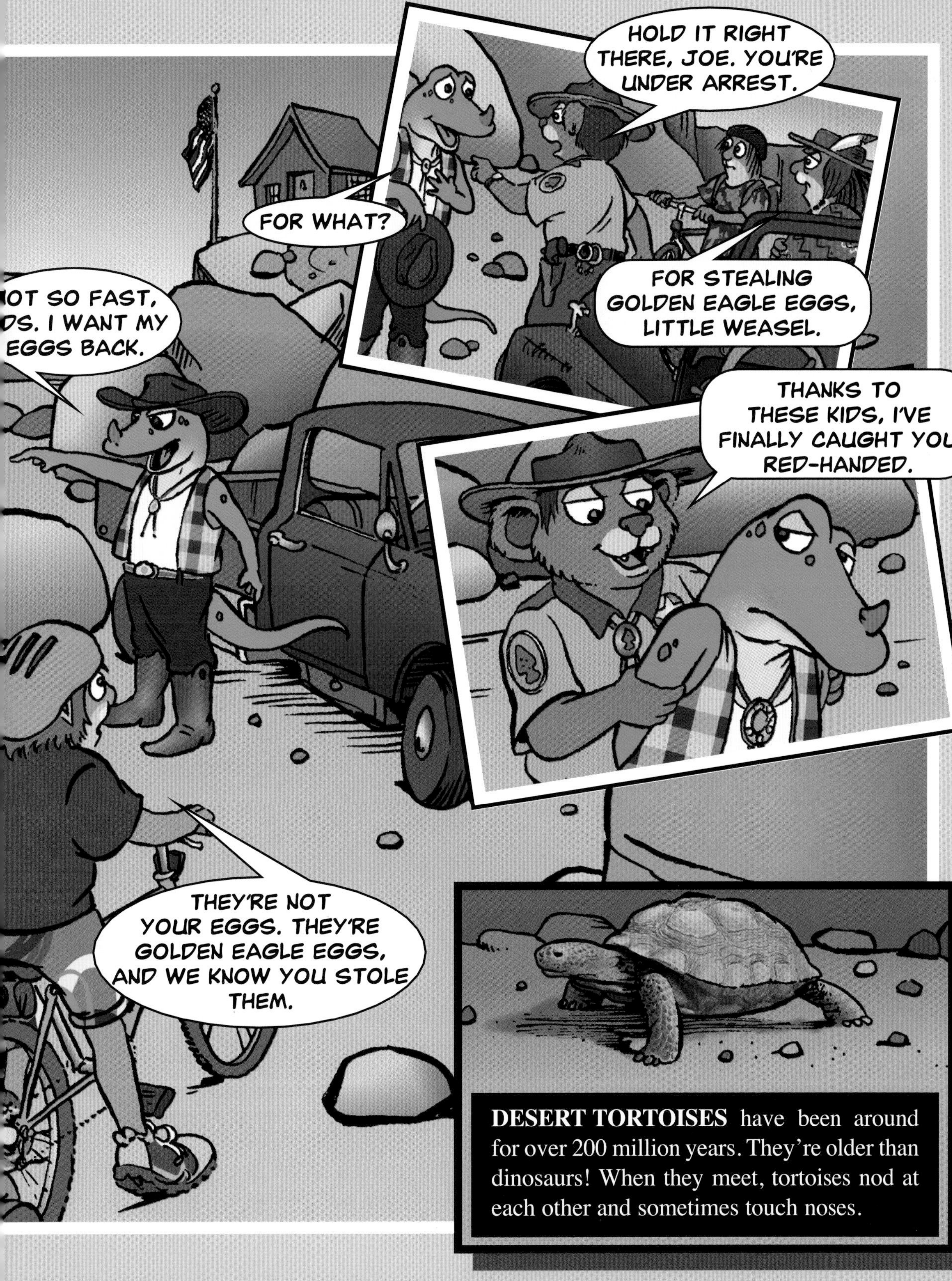
OT SO FAST,
DS. I WANT MY
EGGS BACK.
THEY'RE NOT YOUR EGGS. THEY'RE GOLDEN EAGLE EGGS, AND WE KNOW YOU STOLE THEM.
HOLD IT RIGHT THERE, JOE. YOU'RE UNDER ARREST.
FOR WHAT?
FOR STEALING GOLDEN EAGLE EGGS, LITTLE WEASEL.
THANKS TO THESE KIDS, I'VE FINALLY CAUGHT YOU RED-HANDED.

DESERT TORTOISES have been around for over 200 million years. They're older than dinosaurs! When they meet, tortoises nod at each other and sometimes touch noses.

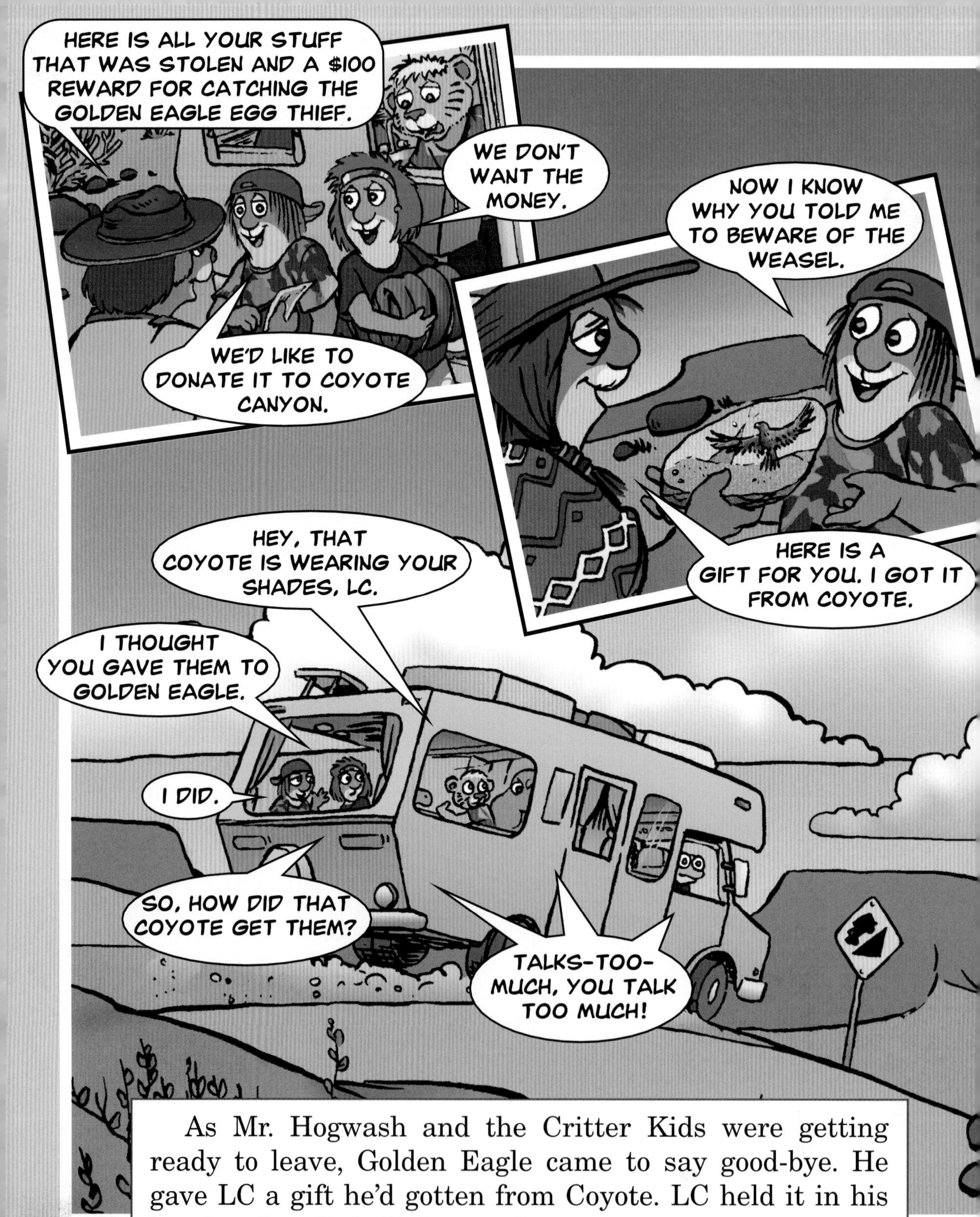
HERE IS ALL YOUR STUFF THAT WAS STOLEN AND A $100 REWARD FOR CATCHING THE GOLDEN EAGLE EGG THIEF.
WE DON'T WANT THE MONEY.
WE'D LIKE TO DONATE IT TO COYOTE CANYON.
NOW I KNOW WHY YOU TOLD ME TO BEWARE OF THE WEASEL.
HERE IS A GIFT FOR YOU. I GOT IT FROM COYOTE.
HEY, THAT COYOTE IS WEARING YOUR SHADES, LC.
I THOUGHT YOU GAVE THEM TO GOLDEN EAGLE.
I DID.
SO, HOW DID THAT COYOTE GET THEM?
TALKS-TOO-MUCH, YOU TALK TOO MUCH!

As Mr. Hogwash and the Critter Kids were getting ready to leave, Golden Eagle came to say good-bye. He gave LC a gift he'd gotten from Coyote. LC held it in his hand and smiled all the way home.

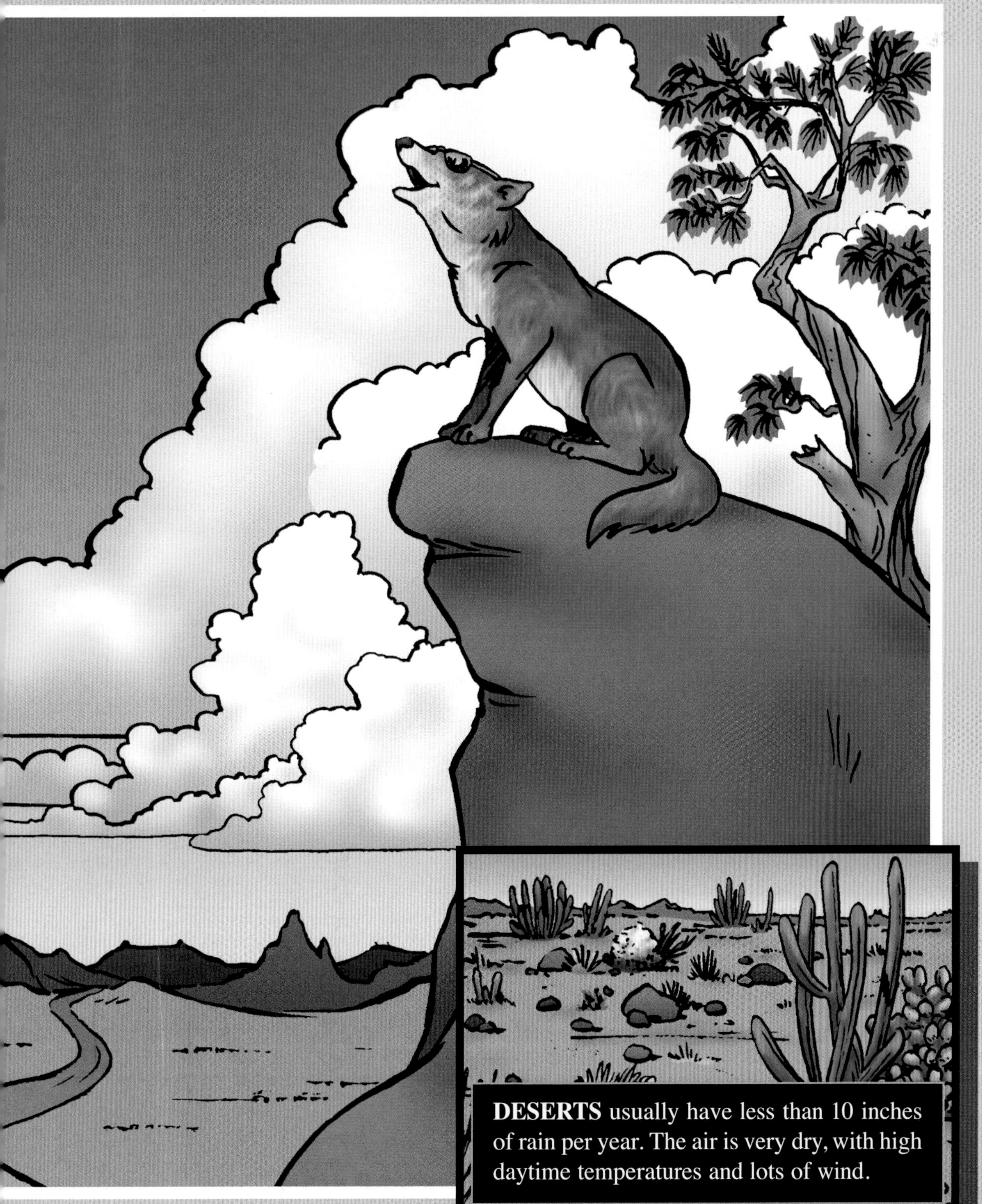

DESERTS usually have less than 10 inches of rain per year. The air is very dry, with high daytime temperatures and lots of wind.

Vocabulary

arachnids—the class of 8-legged animals that includes spiders, scorpions, and mites. *Our class learned that scorpions have 8 legs, just like all arachnids.*

archaeologist—a person who studies how people lived long ago by looking for the objects they may have left behind. *An archaeologist uses special tools when digging for objects.*

canyon—a deep, cliff-sided gorge. *Looking down at the bottom of the steep canyon made me dizzy.*

kindling—small, dry pieces of burnable material used to start a fire. *We gathered lots of twigs for kindling for our campfire.*

nocturnal—occurring at night, rather than during the day. *Coyotes are nocturnal animals that hunt mice and other small animals at night.*

omelet—beaten eggs that are cooked and served folded in half over a filling, such as cheese or ham. *Velvet wanted a western omelet, which is usually made with eggs, diced ham, green pepper, and onion.*

preserve—an area where wildlife is protected. *Who was the thief who stole the golden eagle eggs from the preserve?*

prey—animals that are hunted and killed by other animals for food. *Scorpions use their claws to crush their prey.*

trading post—a store in an isolated area, where local products can be bought or traded for supplies. *Su Su bought jewelry at the trading post during her trip to the desert.*

vision—an image or event seen in a dream or trance that can be interpreted as having future importance. *Golden Eagle predicted that LC would have a vision that would tell him where to find the missing golden eagle eggs.*

The Story and You

What did Gabby mean when she said that Joe gave her "the creeps"? Why did she feel that way about him?

Why were the boot prints unusual?

Why do you think Golden Eagle gave LC a feather?

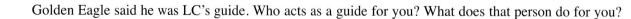

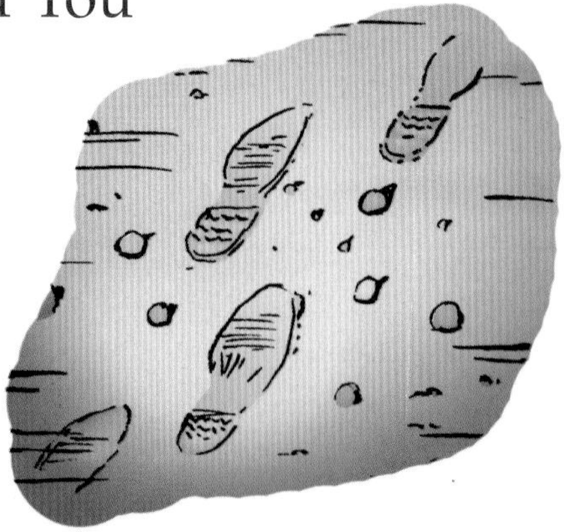

Golden Eagle said he was LC's guide. Who acts as a guide for you? What does that person do for you?